LOVE'S DESTINY

Her face was drawn and haggard; her normally rich pecan-colored skin was pale and dry. But the stress truly showed in her eyes. Red and puffy from crying, her eyes' vacant, lost look revealed the turmoil churning in her soul.

"Oh, baby," he breathed, at a loss for words when she appeared. "Savannah, darling, how are you?"

"I'm scared, Anthony," she answered honestly. "I didn't kill Dwayne, but that doesn't seem to matter. I keep thinking about every story I've ever heard about people who were wrongfully tried and convicted and wound up spending the best years of their lives in jail for a crime they didn't commit. What if that happens to me?"

"It won't happen to you, because I won't let it." Anthony's voice was strong and firm. "I'm going to get you out of this. You have to believe that."

With an effort, she lifted her eyes to meet his.

"I swear to you, I will not rest until I have proven your innocence."

Their eyes stayed locked on each other for several long moments, Savannah drawing strength from Anthony.

"I'm going back to Detroit today," he said finally. "I have some new information that I got from the prosecutor here, and I believe I can track down some evidence in Detroit."

"You're leaving?" Savannah whispered.

"But I'm coming back," he assured her. "And when I do, it'll be to take you home. I give you my word. Do you trust me?"

Savannah managed a nod. "With my life," she said simply.

LOVE'S DESTINY

Crystal Wilson-Harris

ARABESQUE

★BET

BOOKS

BET Publications LLC
http://www.bet.com
http://www.arabesquebooks.com

ARABESQUE BOOKS are published by

BET Publications, LLC
c/o BET BOOKS
One BET Plaza
1900 W Place NE
Washington, DC 20018-1211

All Kensington Titles, Imprints, and Distributed Lines are available at special quantity discounts for bulk purchases for sales promotions, premiums, fund-raising, and educational or institutional use. Special book excerpts or customized printings can also be created to fit specific needs. For details, write or phone the office of the Kensington special sales manager: Kensington Publishing Corp., 850 Third Avenue, New York, NY 10022, attn: Special Sales Department, Phone: 1-800-221-2647.

First Printing: April 2002
10 9 8 7 6 5 4 3 2 1

Printed in the United States of America

For my sister, road-dog, and confidante—Julie Wilson.
Thanks for always having my back. . . .

One

"What are you saying? I don't understand." Savannah Dailey struggled to focus on the irate man standing on the porch in front of her, but her brain was not fully engaged. She pulled her bathrobe closer to her body and shook her head to clear the early morning fog.

"What don't you understand, Mrs. Dailey? My paycheck bounced! I went to the bank first thing this morning and they told me this account had insufficient funds." He spat the words.

"Paul, please calm down. There must be some kind of mistake. . . ."

"Damn right there's some kind of mistake! Look, Mrs. Dailey, I'm sorry to have gotten you out of bed, but this is important. If you and Mr. D think I'm gonna work for free—"

Savannah quickly shook her head. "Don't be ridiculous, Paul. Of course we don't expect you to work for free. There's just been some kind of error at the bank, that's all." She managed a weak smile. "You know how disorganized Saturdays can be down at the bank." She opened the door wider and stepped aside, inviting her employee into the house.

"Let me get Dwayne. He'll be able to straighten all this out."

Apparently reluctant to cross the threshold, Paul grumbled and stepped into the foyer of the Daileys' home. He stood off to the side, his worthless paycheck clutched tightly in his fist.

Savannah cast a sympathetic eye on him. "Dwayne must be out in the shed. I'll get him. You just wait here."

She hurried through the house and out the back door, to her husband's workshop behind the garage. "Dwayne!" She called his name before she reached the shed. "Dwayne! Paul from the shop is here and apparently there is some mix-up at the bank."

There was no answer to her call. Savannah jerked open the shed door. "Dwayne!" The word was packed with annoyance.

Her voice echoed back at her from the empty shed. Only then did Savannah realize that she had heard no sounds of power tools whirring or metal pipes clanging. "Dwayne?" The word was softer, more tentative now. "Where is he?" Some lingering disbelief caused her to flick on the lights. Fluorescent light flooded the shed, starkly illuminating the empty interior. The bright lights glinted off Dwayne's tools, some neatly lined up along his workbench, some hanging from hooks against the wall.

"Where is he?" Savannah snapped off the lights and turned toward the two-car garage. Opening the door, she saw immediately that Dwayne's Chevy Blazer was not in its customary parking space. She heaved a sigh of relief. "He must have already gone to the bank," she reasoned. "He's probably down there right now straightening out this whole mess."

She returned to the house to give the irate employee a status report. When she reached the foyer, she found her fifteen-year-old son engaged in a friendly conversation with Paul.

"Oh, hey, Mom. I heard voices so I got up to see what was going on."

"I knew it had to be something. You never fall out of bed until noon on Saturdays."

Savannah smiled warmly at her son. "D.J., would you excuse me and Paul for a moment? I need to talk to him."

"No problem." D.J. turned toward the kitchen. "See ya later, Mr. Paul."

"You take care, D.J.," Paul called in response. "He's getting tall." Paul directed his comment to Savannah.

"Almost as tall as his daddy." Savannah beamed. "But he's still just a kid, and I have to remind him every now and then that I'm still his momma."

Paul nodded and smiled knowingly. "So where's Mr. D?" The brief respite was over.

"Dwayne's not here," Savannah answered. "He is probably at the bank right now getting this situation resolved. I will have him call you as soon as he gets home."

Paul hesitated, clearly reluctant to leave without his pay in hand.

"Really, Paul, it's all going to be fine. I'll see to it you get your pay in cash if you'd like." Savannah's smile was reassuringly confident. "You know how valuable you are to us. I'm so sorry you had to go through this, but I promise it's all going to be fine."

"I was s'posed to work today. I was trying to cash my check before I went into the shop," Paul said.

"Why don't you go on to the shop? I'm sure Dwayne will go there after he leaves the bank." She laid a gentle hand on Paul's arm. "Paul, you have worked for us for eleven years, ever since there has been a Dailey Plumbing, and this is the first time anything like this has ever happened. I know it's frustrating, but you have to trust Dwayne and me. We always take care of our people. Now go on to work, and this situation will be resolved by lunch."

Paul nodded and appeared to relax. "Thanks, Mrs. Dailey. I'll be at the shop . . . waiting for my money." He turned and left Savannah's home.

As Savannah watched him leave, fragmented, jumbled thoughts whirled about in her mind.

What could have happened? That's not like Dwayne . . . he's usually so meticulous about the books.

She closed the door and went to the kitchen to call her husband's cell phone.

"Everything okay, Mom?" D.J. looked up from the gigantic bowl of cereal he was eating.

"Yes, baby, everything's fine. There's been some mistake down at the bank, but your father is taking care of it."

"The cellular phone you are calling is either turned off or out of the service area. Please try your call again later." The recorded message was terse.

Why doesn't he have his phone on? Savannah's brow crinkled. Shrugging, she decided to wait for her husband to come home with what she was sure would be a simple explanation. She hung up the phone and went to her bedroom to dress.

It was then that she noticed his clothes were missing. Savannah's mind did not immediately register the significance of the freely dangling hangers that rocked gently in the draft created when she opened the closet door. She stared dumbly in the empty space for an interminable moment. Her eyes darted around the closet as her brain finally engaged.

Shoes . . . shirts . . . pants . . . belts . . . She reeled from the shock of it all. Some corner of her psyche that was steeped in denial fought to find a reasonable explanation.

Dry cleaners? Spring cleaning? The words rang stupid and hollow in the rational part of her mind. The shrill of the telephone startled her. She backed away from the closet and stumbled to her nightstand to answer the insistent ringing.

"Yes?" Her voice sounded unfamiliar to her ears.

"Dwayne or Savannah Dailey please." The feminine voice sounded cool and professional.

"This is Savannah Dailey." She wrenched her eyes from the empty closet to try and focus on the phone call.

"Mrs. Dailey, this is the bank calling about the Dailey Plumbing payroll account—"

"Yes, I'm glad you called." Happy to have something else to focus on, Savannah interrupted the woman. "One of my employees was here this morning complaining that his paycheck bounced. What are you people doing down there?"

"Uh, Mrs. Dailey, there has been some kind of mistake—" the woman began.

"Yes, there has. My husband and I have been doing business with your bank for years, and we expect to be treated better than this." Savannah's tone had gotten hard. "Now whatever the mix-up is, I expect my people to be paid."

"Mrs. Dailey, the payroll account has a zero balance."

"That's not possible," Savannah stammered.

"I'm sorry, it is." The bank woman was firm. "Several of your employees have tried to cash checks today, and we had to refuse them all. The branch manager suggested calling you or your husband. He thought maybe you forgot to make a deposit?"

"That seems unlikely." Savannah's mind raced to find an answer. "Until I can speak to my husband and get this straightened out, just transfer funds from the primary business account to cover the payroll."

"Um . . ." The woman hesitated. "We can't do that."

"Why?" Savannah's question was shrill.

"Well, when we realized the payroll account was empty, we checked the primary account. Mrs. Dailey, it's empty, too."

Savannah's jaw fell open and her eyes shot back to the empty closet. "Our personal account?" The question reeked with dread.

"I'm so sorry, Mrs. Dailey. The personal account has a zero balance also." The banker's voice was sympathetic.

Savannah felt her entire body freeze, as if somehow ice water had replaced the blood in her veins. The phone receiver slipped from her nerveless fingers and clattered against the nightstand on its way to the floor.

Dwayne . . . what have you done?

Savannah collapsed into a formless heap on the floor as merciful blackness closed in around her.

Two

"Savannah, honey, speak to me." The words were accompanied by a gentle but insistent patting on Savannah's cheeks. Slowly Savannah returned to the light and began to focus on the face above her.

"Paris?" She whispered the name. "What are you doing here? What happened?"

Paris Raven helped her sister up into a sitting position. "D.J. and Stephanie called me. They were terrified to find their mom passed out on the floor. Savannah, what happened?" Paris's look shifted between Savannah and the kids. "Where's Dwayne?"

"We tried to call him on his cell phone," D.J. interjected, "but it was turned off."

Savannah lowered her head and leaned in closer. "I can't talk in front of the kids," she hissed.

Clearly confused, Paris yielded to her sister's wishes. She turned to her niece and nephew, who hovered near the door, a poignant combination of worry and fear etched on their faces.

"It's okay guys. Your mom is fine." Paris managed a reassuring smile. "Now could you give us a minute please?"

D.J. and his thirteen-year-old sister Stephanie hesitated. "Mom? Are you sure you're okay?" Stephanie took a tentative step in her mother's direction. "We were so scared. We didn't know what to do."

"I'm fine, babies, really. Just had a little dizzy spell, that's all." Savannah rose from her seated position with some difficulty. "You did the right thing calling your Aunt Paris." She went to the children and pulled them into a hug. "I love you both so much." Her voice caught on the words.

"Mom? What's wrong?" D.J.'s tone was insistent. "Are you sick or something?"

"No, sweetie," Savannah was quick to reassure him. "I'm not sick." She released them from the hug and gently guided them out the door. "Now just give me a few minutes with Aunt Paris, okay?"

Though obviously relieved that their mother seemed fine, the teens were reluctant to leave her side. Eventually, they backed out of the room, leaving Savannah and her sister alone.

"C'mon, Savannah. What gives?" Paris pounced as soon as the bedroom door closed behind the kids.

Savannah shook her head wearily. "I don't know what's going on," she began. "Something's happening with Dwayne . . ."

"Something like what? Is he sick?"

"Well, that's one possible explanation." Savannah's words were dry and humorless. "Insanity maybe."

"What are you talking about?" Paris looked at her older sister curiously.

In answer, Savannah stalked over to the closet and jerked the door open. "Look," she demanded. "See anything missing?"

Paris turned to face the empty closet. "I don't understand . . ." she started.

"Don't understand? Well, take a number in that line." Savannah stormed across the room to a tall chest of drawers in the corner. "I didn't even think to look in here." She snatched the handle with such force that the mostly empty drawer came all the way out of the frame. She stared dumbly at the smattering of socks and worn briefs that fluttered to the floor. "Of course, all his good drawers are missing . . . these he left behind."

"Behind?" Paris's brow creased in question.

"That's right, Paris—behind! Dwayne has gone and left me with angry employees, empty bank accounts, and his raggedy underwear." Savannah snatched some of the white cotton briefs from the floor and flung them across the room. "How could he do this to me? And how could I not know what was going on?" She teetered on the edge of hysteria.

"Savannah, calm down." Paris held her hands in front of her like a shield as she approached her sister. "I'm sure there's just been some kind of misunderstanding. Dwayne wouldn't do that. He wouldn't just leave like that."

"Misunderstanding!" The word exploded from Savannah. "What part do you think I misunderstood, Paris? The missing clothes? Dry cleaners—right?" Sarcasm filled the words as Savannah paced around the room like a caged jungle cat. "Maybe you think I wasn't clear about the zero-balance bank accounts . . . or the payroll checks that are bouncing all over town."

Paris stood in shocked silence for a moment. "It's got to be something else, Savannah. Dwayne wouldn't do that to his family. Dwayne is the most levelheaded, responsible man I know."

"Guess that just goes to show you never really know a person."

"Honey, what are you saying?" Paris studied her sister closely.

"I mean I knew things were strained between us, but all married couples go through rough patches." Savannah spoke as if she had forgotten Paris was in the room. "But never in my wildest nightmares had I ever imagined he would do something like this." Savannah plopped down heavily in the center of the floor and buried her face in her hands. "Dwayne"— her voice was muffled by sobs—"what have you done?"

Paris stood helplessly watching her sister's anguish. Jumbled thoughts coursed through her mind. *There has to be some explanation . . . something other than the obvious.* Her rational and emotional sides warred for dominance. *Savannah and Dwayne were the perfect couple with the perfect family and the perfect life. How does something like this happen?*

The phone rang, breaking into Paris's thoughts, demanding attention. Since Savannah was still in a heap on the floor, Paris grabbed the instrument.

"Hello?"

"Let me speak to Mr. Dailey. This is Paul from the shop." Paul's voice projected his impatience.

"Mr. Dailey is not here right now," Paris hedged, "I'll tell him you called."

"Wait a minute—let me talk to Mrs. Dailey," Paul insisted.

Paris looked over at her sister, who was still crying softly into her hands. "Uh, she can't come to the phone right now. I will give her a message."

"Fine," Paul snapped, "give her this message. Tell

her the guys here at the shop want their money. Tell her we ain't gonna wait much longer. Tell her if we don't get our money soon, we're walking outta here." Paul paused, allowing an ominous silence to build. "And her and Mr. D need to know some of the guys are talking about taking the equipment to sell if they don't get paid." Paul hung up the phone without waiting for a reply.

Paris stared dumbly at the phone in her hand, the dial tone only faintly registering in her mind. Instead, her ears still rang from the angry, threatening words that ended the call: ". . . taking the equipment to sell . . ."

Slowly, Paris replaced the receiver in its cradle. She turned to Savannah. "Honey, it was Paul from the shop," she started. "It's not looking good—the guys are getting impatient."

Unexpectedly, a harsh laugh erupted from Savannah. "Not looking good, huh, Paris? Ya think?" Almost as soon as the words left her mouth, Savannah started crying again. "I'm so sorry, sweetie," she apologized through her tears. "There is no reason for me to go off on you." She went to her sister and hugged her. "Oh, God, Paris, what am I going to do?"

Ever the practical Raven sister, Paris was already working on a plan. With deliberate slowness, she picked up the phone. She turned a stern but compassionate gaze on her oldest sister. "I'm going to call her."

At first, there was only a blank questioning look on Savannah's face. Then realization dawned. "No." She shook her head. "Not her."

"Savannah, you have no choice! You need money,

and you need it now. She's the only person we know with the kind of money you need." Paris was adamant.

"I don't think I can bear it," Savannah whined. "She'll just lord it over me like she always does. This'll just make her day."

"Savannah, you're being silly. Sydney is our sister. She will be happy to help you out."

"Oh, yeah, she'll be happy all right . . . happy 'cause she can gloat and act superior."

"I don't think you're being fair to Syd, but in any case, you need her help. I'm going to call."

"Paris, wait. There has to be another way. Give me a minute to think."

Paris's mouth turned down in a disapproving frown. "While you're thinking, think about this. It's more than just you who needs help. Those kids out there are going to be traumatized by all this. You owe it to them to keep their lives as normal as possible. Savannah, if you won't call Sydney for yourself, call her for them."

Savannah's shoulders slumped in defeat. "That was a low blow, Paris."

"Maybe, but that doesn't make it any less true." Paris began pushing buttons on the phone. "I'm making the call."

Sydney Raven was heading for her front door when the phone rang. "Not now," she muttered. "I'm already late for my hair appointment." She was on the verge of ignoring the summons when she checked the caller ID box next to the phone. "Sa-

vannah?" Instantly, Sydney's curiosity was piqued.
She answered.

"Savannah?" Her tone rang with question.

"No, Syd. It's Paris."

Sydney's delicately arched brows furrowed. "Hey,
Paris. What you doing at Savannah's house?"

There was a brief pause. "Savannah's in trouble,
Syd. And she needs your help."

"Is that right? What kind of trouble?" Sydney
placed a hand on her hip.

"Just come over, Syd. We need to talk to you."

"We? I thought you said Savannah was in trouble?
Besides, I was just on my way to Andre's to get my
hair done. I'll stop by after my appointment."

"Now, Sydney. Come now." Paris's tone invited no
further discussion.

Reluctant but responding to the urgency in Paris's
voice, Sydney relented. "On my way."

As she drove to her older sister's house, Sydney's
mind raced. *What could it be? Paris sounded seriously
upset. And why didn't Savannah ask me for help herself?*

"Okay, what's the emergency?" Sydney breezed
into Savannah's house.

"Hi, Aunt Sydney," Stephanie greeted her first.
"What cha doin' here?"

Sydney hugged her niece warmly. "I don't know,
kiddo. Your Aunt Paris called and said I had to get
over here. She said there was some kind of emergency."

"Emergency?" The smile melted off of Stephanie's face. "They said Momma was fine. What's go-

ing on, Aunt Syd? Why are you here? Where's my daddy?"

"Baby, I don't know yet. But I'm sure everything's all right." Sydney tried to calm her niece. "Where are your mom and Aunt Paris?"

"They've been closed up in Momma's room ever since Momma passed out."

"Passed out?" Sydney struggled not to show her concern, not wanting to upset Stephanie any further. "Well, let me go back there and I'll find out what's going on. Don't worry, baby, Aunt Sydney will take care of it."

Sydney knocked once, then threw open Savannah's bedroom door. "What on earth is going on here? Stephanie just told me Savannah passed out. Are you sick or something?"

"Hello to you too, Sydney," Savannah said dryly. "Why don't you close the door so we can talk?"

Frowning, Sydney did as she was bid. "Come on, somebody give. What's the emergency that had me racing all the way out here to the boondocks?"

Savannah snorted. "Sorry, Syd. Everybody can't afford to live downtown in a dee-luxe apartment in the sky."

"Don't start." Paris stepped between her sisters "Now is not the time."

"Okay, Paris." Sydney looked at her. "What is it time for?"

"Savannah, do you want to tell her or do you want me to?"

Savannah waved her hand dismissively as she crossed the room to sit on her bed.

Sydney's head turned from one sister to the other. "Well, somebody tell me something."

Paris took a deep breath. "Sydney, it appears Dwayne has left."

Sydney's eyes widened. "What do you mean left?"

Paris shrugged. "I mean *left*. He took all his clothes—"

"Except for his raggedy underwear," Savannah interjected bitterly. "Don't forget that part. He left his raggedy underwear and work clothes."

Sydney leaned against the wall for support. "But you and Dwayne were so happy. Savannah, are you sure he left? I mean, couldn't it be something else?" Sydney turned a pleading look on her oldest sister. "Dwayne wouldn't do that to his family."

"Believe me, Syd, you're not saying anything I haven't said to myself over and over again this morning. But the facts remain the same . . . Dwayne's clothes and car are gone. And all our bank accounts are empty."

"What?" The word exploded from Sydney's lips.

"Yep, that's right." Savannah looked away. "On his way out, Dwayne stopped by the bank and made a little withdrawal."

"That's why I called Sydney," Paris said. "Savannah needs money, a lot of it, and fast. Dwayne took the money out of the payroll account. Their employees are threatening to sell the plumbing equipment if they don't get paid soon."

"I don't know what to say." Sydney rubbed her temples. "Savannah, are you all right?"

"Syd, I don't even know what that means anymore." Savannah's voice was drained of emotion.

"Sydney, can you help with the money?" Paris persisted.

"How much money are we talking about?"

"Enough to cover this week's payroll and some living expenses for Savannah and the kids."

"For how long?"

Paris looked to Savannah. "What do you think?"

"I don't know what I think." The hysteria Savannah had managed to control threatened to resurface. "I don't know when I'll be able to pay you back because I don't know what's going on with the business. Dwayne always took care of the business and I took care of the house and the kids. That was our deal! And now, I don't know what I'm going to do." Savannah buried her face in her hands. "I'm thirty-eight years old and I entrusted my entire life and future to my husband. Everything I was and everything I had I poured into this marriage and this family, and look where it's gotten me. Alone with a stack of bills and a pile of raggedy underwear!"

And then the tears came again. Great, wracking sobs that seemed to start from the depths of her soul and reverberate through her body until she shuddered from their force. Sydney and Paris encircled their sister, lending her their strength. For a few intensely emotional minutes, the Raven sisters cried together, mourning the loss of the family they had come to count on and the life they had come to expect.

Then Sydney took charge.

"Of course I'll get the money for you. But I can't get to my bank until Monday, so we'll have to handle the guys at the shop."

"I can take care of that," Paris said.

"Good." Sydney was mentally preparing a battle plan. "Savannah, you'll have to get the business's accounting books and see what your status is . . . who you owe money to and who owes money to you. You're going to have to collect any outstanding invoices."

"Syd, I don't know if I can," Savannah began.

"Savannah, I don't know if you have any choice," Sydney insisted. "Even if you decide to sell the business, you'll still need to fully understand the financial picture."

Savannah nodded sullenly.

"And here's the last thing." Sydney reached for her purse. "We're going to hire a private detective to find Dwayne and make him pay back what he stole. And I'm not talking only money."

Savannah's head shot up. "You can't be serious! Hire a detective to find Dwayne? Why on earth would I want to find Dwayne?"

"Why on earth wouldn't you? Savannah, this was a cowardly thing to do to people he claimed to love, and Dwayne has to be made to account for it."

"I don't ever want to see him again. I don't care if he's found."

"Savannah, I'm pretty sure that beyond breaking your heart and betraying his family, Dwayne has broken the law. He can't be allowed to get away with it." Sydney dug around in her purse and produced a business card. "This guy is a private detective we've used at my company once or twice. He's very good. I'm going to call him and ask him to come over. We've got to start looking for Dwayne before the trail gets too cold."

Savannah shook her head. "I don't want to find Dwayne! You're right, this was a cowardly thing to do to his family, and if he doesn't care any more about us than that, I say let him stay wherever he is . . . we don't need him."

"This isn't about needing him," Sydney insisted. "This is about justice. Now I'm making the call."

"Sydney, don't," Savannah tried again.

"Savannah, if you want my help, you'll talk to this detective and let him do his job."

"Wait a minute." Savannah put up her hand. "Are you saying the only way you'll lend me the money is if I let you hire this detective to hunt Dwayne down?"

Sydney paused for a moment. "I wouldn't have said it like that—"

"But that's what you mean, right?" Savannah whirled to face Paris, who had been quietly watching the exchange between her sisters. "See, I told you," Savannah said. "Her help never comes without strings attached. This is even worse than the gloating I expected."

"The gloating you expected?" Sydney was shocked. "You expected me to gloat over this situation? What kind of a person do you think I am?"

"But this is worse than gloating," Savannah continued as if she hadn't heard Sydney speak. "This is controlling. This is Sydney the generous telling me what I have to do to earn her help."

"Somebody needs to tell you what to do," Sydney snapped. "Clearly you aren't doing so great a job on your own."

"All right, that's enough!" Paris stepped into her customary role as peacemaker. "Both of you stop it before you say something you can't take back. This has been one helluva stressful day for everybody, and I think we all need to just take a deep breath and calm down."

Paris reached for each sister's hand and held them tightly together. "Now listen, you two. This is a time of crisis; this is the time when we stick together to make it through. Whatever petty differences or disagreements you had in the past don't matter now. All that matters now is that we do whatever has to be done to hold our family together. Now, Savannah, Sydney is right. Dwayne does have to be found. Let this detective take care of that while you focus on putting your life back together."

After a deep breath, Savannah nodded. "You're right of course. Sydney, please accept my apologies. I've been hateful to you ever since you walked into this room. I guess I'm just scared . . ." Her voice trailed off. "But that's no excuse." She reached for Sydney's free hand so that all three sisters formed a circle with their clasped hands.

"Thank you for coming to my rescue," Savannah said. I don't know what I'd do without my sisters."

Sydney kissed Savannah's cheek. "I'm just glad I can help."

Paris nodded, satisfied. "I'm going to try and find Jakarta."

"Why?" Sydney and Savannah asked the question in unison.

"Because our baby sister deserves to know what's going on. She'll want to be here, too." Paris shook her head, cutting off any farther objections. "We all have things we need to get started on. Sydney, call the detective."

Savannah nodded her agreement.

Three

That phone was not supposed to ring. The thought flashed through Anthony Martin's mind. *The whole reason I came in on Saturday was that it was supposed to be quiet so I could get some paperwork done.* He glared at the instrument, debating between answering it and allowing his voice mail to pick up. *It's probably a wrong number,* he rationalized. *But then again, it could be business . . . and if somebody's calling on a Saturday, it must be important.*

Disgusted at himself for his apparent inability to ignore a ringing phone, Anthony grabbed the receiver just before the voice mail was set to click on.

"Martin Investigations. Anthony Martin speaking."

"Yes, hello. This is Sydney Raven. I have a situation I'd like to speak with you about."

Anthony allowed himself a brief, smug smile. *See?* he thought. *Business. Good thing I answered.*

"How can I help you, Ms. Raven?" He adopted his most professional tone.

"It's a very sensitive matter, Mr. Martin. I'd appreciate it if you could come to my sister's house so we could discuss the matter in person."

Anthony hesitated, looking at the pile of paperwork on his desk. "Can you give me some sense of what you need?"

Sydney sighed impatiently. "I would really prefer not to get into it over the phone," she insisted. "I can tell you it's a missing person case."

"Missing person? Perhaps you should call the police."

"Um . . . no," Sydney said. "We don't want to involve the police if it can be avoided."

"I see. Yes, of course, I'll be right over." Anthony reached for a pen. "What's the address?" He made note of the address and directions and replaced the phone on its hook.

Anthony rose from his behind his desk and walked to the small bathroom off to the side of his office. He pulled his polo-style shirt over his head and tossed it onto the closed lid of the toilet. At twenty-eight, Anthony Martin was in peak physical condition. His smooth chest was well defined, the product of thrice weekly workouts at the gym and a regular Wednesday night basketball game with his friends. His rich toasted almond coloring, soft brown hair that lay in gentle waves along his scalp, and startlingly green eyes had caused more than one person, some privately and some directly, to question his ethnicity.

Whenever asked, Anthony proudly declared himself the biracial only child of a second-generation Italian-American mother and an African-American father. He'd always felt equally at home in both cultures, moving easily between his loud and loving Italian family to his loud and loving black family. He had always been grateful that both sides of his family accepted his parents and their decision to marry despite the challenges they would face.

His decision to become a detective had been an easy one. He had briefly considered following in his father's footsteps to become a Detroit police officer. But ultimately, Anthony decided he'd find more challenge and more independence as a private investigator. And he was one of the best. With his contacts in the police department and on the streets, Anthony was very well tuned into the pulse of the city. His youth and boyish face masked a quick mind and a steely determination to see a case through to its resolution.

As he prepared to go meet with his newest client, he quickly splashed water on his face and wiped with a nearby washcloth. He turned from the basin to get the spare shirt and tie he kept for occasions like this, hanging on a hook on the back of the bathroom door. Quickly shrugging into the shirt, he loosely tied the tie around his neck and tucked the shirttails into his jeans. Although he would have preferred not to meet a client in jeans, it was Saturday, and he didn't have time to stop home and change. He checked himself one last time in the mirror. Deciding he was presentable, Anthony grabbed his briefcase and headed out of the office.

In his car on the way across town, Anthony began processing what he already knew and what he could deduce about this new case.

This missing person is either a business partner or a wayward husband, he decided. *The woman didn't sound frantic enough for it to be a child. There's most likely some money missing too . . . and she wants to keep it quiet; that's why she's called me and not the police.* He checked the address he'd scrawled on a scrap of paper. *Nice neighborhood. Sydney Raven said this was her sister's house. The missing person must belong to her sister. Wonder why the sister didn't make the call?* Anthony considered the dynamics of the case. *Well, it ought to be interesting at the very least,* he concluded. *Certainly more interesting than a desk full of paperwork.*

He slowed as he approached the street he'd been directed to. He made the turn and began looking for the address. Shortly, he found the right house and parked on the street in front. The house was an English Tudor-style two-level. It was large, but not the largest on the street. Anthony noticed a two-car detached garage and a work shed off to the side of the house, both structures boasting a Tudor construction that echoed the main house. He made a mental note of the cars in the driveway—a shiny red BMW sedan and a sturdy, sensible white Ford Taurus. He straightened his tie, grabbed his briefcase off the floor of the car, and headed up the brick walkway to meet the day's newest challenge.

Anthony pushed the doorbell and listened as chimes rang throughout the house. After a few moments, the door opened and Anthony found himself face-to-face with a sullen-looking teenaged boy whose age he estimated to be between fourteen and sixteen.

"Hello." Anthony used his most professional, nonthreatening voice. "My name is Anthony Martin and I have an appointment to see Sydney Raven."

Anthony wondered what the boy's attitude was about, but before the thought had fully jelled in his mind, the young man spoke.

"You must be the guy they called to find my dad," the boy said, disgustedly raking his eyes over Anthony.

Anthony didn't respond, choosing instead to watch the boy closely.

"They're all wrong, you know," D.J. continued. "They think Dad's gone but he hasn't. There's something else going on."

Again, Anthony chose not to respond.

"Mom and 'em are in the living room." D.J. turned and left the door opened for Anthony to follow. With a slight shrug, Anthony entered the house, closed the door, and followed the teenager to the living room. In the room, he was immediately struck by the similarities of the three women who looked up to greet him.

"You must be Anthony Martin. I'm Sydney Raven . . . we talked on the phone." Sydney crossed the room and extended her hand to shake.

"Yes, hello, Ms. Raven." Anthony firmly grasped her extended hand. He noticed immediately that Sydney Raven appeared to be the most sophisticated of the three. Her nails were carefully manicured, and two separate bands of diamond tennis bracelets dangled from her slim wrist. He noticed her shoes. Anthony always noticed shoes; it was one of the ways he judged people. Her shoes were designer, he was sure. Even though they were flat loafers, they were clearly designer. *Prada or Aigner,* he thought. She was pretty, but in a hard kind of way, like life had made her cynical. Her dark brown hair was arranged in a neat pageboy that stopped at her chin, and even though it was early Saturday afternoon, her makeup had been carefully applied to impress. Anthony took all this in in an instant, as he'd been trained to do in his profession.

"Your directions were impeccable, Ms. Raven," he said. "I got here with no trouble at all."

"Good, I'm glad to hear that," Sydney said. "Let me introduce my sisters. This is Paris Raven."

Anthony nodded at the plump young woman who sat in an overstuffed chair to his left. She was younger than Sydney, he guessed, but not much . . . three or four years at most. Slightly darker brown than her honey-colored sister, Paris Raven was the kind of woman about whom people always said in well-meaning and sympathetic tones, "She has such a pretty face . . . if only she would lose weight." Her shoes, Anthony noticed, were sensible flat walking shoes. Thinking back at the cars in the driveway, he decided that the BMW belonged to Ms. Prada shoes, and the Ford Taurus belonged to Ms. Rockport.

"It's a pleasure to meet you, Ms. Raven." Anthony smiled at Paris. Paris nodded.

"And this is my sister Savannah." Sydney turned and walked to a chair on the other side of the room. She rested her arm along the back of the chair, touching the chair, but not her sister. "Savannah Raven Dailey."

"Hello, Mrs. Dailey?" Anthony said with a question in his tone.

"Yes." Savannah nodded. "Mrs. Dailey will be fine. After all, I'm Mrs. Dailey . . . or I was Mrs. Dailey . . . I guess I'm still Mrs. Dailey . . ." Her voice trailed off for a moment. "Oh, hell, call me Savannah," she huffed finally.

Savannah was clearly the oldest of the Raven sisters. The red in her eyes revealed a bit of the trauma that she had endured that day. Her hair hung loose and rested along her shoulders. It was full and thick and shiny, almost in defiance of the dull gray pallor that tinged her face. As Anthony looked closer, he could see the tracks in her scalp that indicated a hair weave, and he wondered—briefly—why she chose to wear a weave. Savannah sat slumped in the chair, curled with her knees drawn to her chest. A rich pecan color, Savannah was the middle ground between her walnut-brown sister Paris and her honey-brown sister Sydney.

Sydney took charge of the meeting. "Have a seat, Mr. Martin," she instructed, waving toward the couch. "There's a lot we need to do, and we need you to get started right away."

Anthony sat, opened his briefcase, retrieved a white, legal-sized pad and a pen, situated himself, and prepared to take notes. "How can I help, Ms. Raven?" He addressed Sydney.

"My sister's husband is gone," Sydney said without preamble. "She woke up this morning and he was gone, his car was gone, and their bank accounts were empty."

Savannah, Anthony noticed, flinched away from her sister's harsh telling of the situation and curled even further into a ball.

"Oh, I see," Anthony said in his most professional tone. "Do you have any information at all about where he could have gone?" He still addressed Sydney, sensing that Savannah was not ready to talk about it.

"No," Sydney said. "So far we have nothing."

"Except a mountain of raggedy underwear," Savannah snapped. "Don't forget that. We have his raggedy underwear. You have any bloodhounds at your office, Mr. Martin? We could give the underwear to the bloodhounds so they could track him down." The words dripped pained sarcasm.

"Savannah," Paris said, dismayed. "Please, we all agreed this was the right thing to do. You have to help Mr. Martin do his job."

"I thought I was helping," Savannah said flatly.

Anthony silently watched the interplay between the sisters.

"Savannah, this is difficult enough without the attitude," Sydney said.

Savannah puffed up as if preparing a scathing response, but then just as quickly her mood changed, and she calmed down.

"Yeah, okay." She sighed. "I don't know where he is, Mr. Martin. I didn't know he was planning to go. I looked for him this morning when our employees' checks started to bounce and I discovered he was gone."

"Okay," Anthony said. "Does he have any credit cards? We can trace him through those."

Savannah nodded and produced a sheet of paper. "I've written all of our credit card numbers; the make, model, and license of his truck is on here as well. Anything I could think of that might help you find him. Although I don't know why we're looking for him."

"Because he has to be held accountable," Sydney said emphatically. "He cannot be allowed to get away with this. He has to pay back what he's stolen."

Savannah cut her eyes at her sister, who still stood behind her chair. "It's all about the money, isn't it, Syd?"

Sydney sighed. "It is most immediately about the money. It's not *all* about the money, but it is *certainly* about the money. He has to pay you back, he has to pay the employees back, he has to pay your creditors back."

"And beyond the money, Savannah, don't you want to know why?" Paris asked. "I mean, don't you want to know what would make Dwayne do something like this?"

Savannah shrugged. "I don't know what I want," she said. She uncurled her body from the chair and rose to leave the room. "You all do whatever you think is best. I don't want to deal with this any more today."

Anthony stood respectfully as Savannah left. He watched her smooth movements with admiration; he was impressed by how well she seemed to be handling this most devastating betrayal. He had worked with enough wives of cheating husbands to know that hysterics and raw emotions were the typical reactions. Savannah Raven Dailey, he noted, seemed very controlled—angry and hurt, certainly—but controlled.

"I'll get started right away," Anthony said. "I will find him."

Sydney and Paris nodded in unison. "The sooner the better," Sydney said.

Four

"What do you mean Dwayne left?" The question was shrill and harsh.

"How many different ways are there to mean that, Jakarta?" Paris said impatiently. "Savannah woke up one morning and discovered Dwayne was gone. All his clothes, his car, and all the money out of their accounts."

Jakarta Raven sat back against the headboard of the motel bed, stunned by her older sister's words. "How could he? What the hell was he thinking?"

"Believe me, baby, that's something we'd all like to know."

"How are Savannah and the kids?"

"About how you'd expect," Paris said. "In shock . . . trying to hold it all together."

Jakarta shook her head. "When did all this happen?"

Paris paused. "It's been almost two weeks," she said finally.

"Two weeks! Why am I just now hearing about this?" Jakarta demanded.

"Nobody knew where to find you, J," Paris shot back. "You are good for disappearing off the face of the earth. It took me until now to find you. And I had to call two of your former employers and three of your ex-boyfriends before I could get a message to you. I'm just relieved you decided to respond to my message."

Jakarta rubbed wearily at her eyes. "Don't start with me, Paris . . ."

"You started it, Jakarta. You started it when you decided to go AWOL from your family. But none of that matters now." Paris's tone changed abruptly. "What matters now is that your sister needs you. So you need to get here."

The phone line hummed for a few tension-filled moments as Jakarta silently processed her sister's words. "Come home . . . back to Detroit? Paris, I don't know. . . ."

"Yeah, well, I do." Paris was definitive. "Savannah needs you, and you need to be here. Whatever you've been running from doesn't matter anymore. Your family is the only thing that matters."

"Maybe my family is what I'm running from," Jakarta mumbled under her breath.

"What?" Paris pretended not to hear.

"Never mind." Jakarta sighed. "I'll be there as soon as I can."

Anthony Martin was frustrated. He had been confident that tracking down Dwayne Dailey would be a simple task. Most wayward husbands, in his experience, did not have any real stealth skills. They usually made clumsy mistakes that made tracking them down easy work. Dwayne Dailey, however, was being much more careful than most. In the two weeks Anthony had been on the case, all he had turned up was a series of dead ends.

"What's your story, Dailey?" Anthony mused aloud as he sat at his desk with the case file spread out in front of him. "Why'd you do it? Where'd you go?" Anthony scanned through the documents on the desk, looking for some clue he may have overlooked. "It's more than just an affair, isn't it? Men don't usually clean out their family and business bank accounts just for an affair. Gambling debts? Blackmail payments?" Anthony's brow furrowed as he considered the possibilities.

The Dailey case had taken priority over the other assignments he was working on. He wanted to find Dwayne Dailey and bring him to justice more than he had wanted anything in a long time.

This man is the worst kind of snake there is, Anthony thought. *He had what every man dreams of—a beautiful home, a successful business, and a great family and he threw it all away.*

Anthony pushed away from his desk and stood to stretch the kinks out of his back. His mind conjured up images of Savannah Raven Dailey the one and only time he had seen her. He still remembered and was impressed by her outward calm. It was her sister, Sydney Raven, who had struck Anthony as being the most anxious to find Dwayne. Savannah's attitude was clearly *que sera, sera*—whatever will be, will be.

The strident ringing of the phone interrupted his thoughts. "Anthony Martin," he answered.

"Mr. Martin, this is Sydney Raven. I was calling for an update on the search for my brother-in-law."

Who knew I had the power to summon a person with only my thoughts? Anthony thought wryly. *Now if only it worked with Dailey.*

"Hello, Ms. Raven," he said. "I'm afraid I don't

have much news yet. Your brother-in-law is being very stealthy."

"Well, I don't have to tell you how disappointed I am to hear that," Sydney replied. "I thought you understood the importance and urgency of this matter."

"Oh, I understand, believe me." Anthony decided to broach a subject that had been taboo ever since this investigation started. "Ms. Raven, do you suppose it would be okay if I contacted your sister Savannah directly? I've only been working with you, and I have a sense that if I could talk to her directly about her husband, I may be able to get some information that would be useful."

"Oh, I don't know about that." Sydney was obviously hesitant. "Savannah has made it very clear that she doesn't want to be involved in this investigation."

"Yes, I know, but quite honestly, I don't understand why. The quickest way for this investigation to conclude successfully would be for your sister to cooperate fully." Anthony hoped his frustration didn't show in his voice.

"I know." Sydney sighed. "And I've tried to convince Savannah, but she is just not trying to hear that. She has been totally immersed in trying to take care of her children and hold her business together. To her, finding Dwayne is simply not that high a priority."

"Maybe I could try to convince her. With your permission of course." Anthony was very conscious of who was paying his fee.

"Sure," Sydney agreed. "If you think it will help, give her a call. You have her number, right?"

"Yes, I do," Anthony said. "I'll call her today. I'll try to be as delicate as possible."

"Thank you for that consideration," Sydney said, "but remember our primary goal is to track Dwayne down. And if that means you have to ruffle my sister's feathers a little bit, then that's what has to be done."

"I understand. I'll let you know my progress," Anthony assured her.

"Fine. I'll wait to hear from you." Sydney hung up the phone.

Anthony took a moment to gather his thoughts, trying to decide what would be the best thing to say to Savannah. Once he was prepared, he made the call.

"Hello?" The word was crisp and efficient. Anthony was struck by how strong her voice sounded.

"Savannah Dailey please."

"This is Savannah," she said. "Who's calling?"

"Mrs. Dailey, this is Anthony Martin. I'm the detective your sister hired to find your husband."

Savannah didn't respond.

"I wondered if I could have a few minutes of your time," Anthony charged on.

"Do you have some news for me, Mr. Martin?"

"Actually, no, Mrs. Dailey, I don't. That's why I wanted to talk to you—"

"First of all," Savannah interrupted him, "this will be a much more productive conversation if you stop calling me Mrs. Dailey. I have stopped calling myself that . . . and I have stopped responding to that. So please don't call me Mrs. Dailey."

"I apologize, Mrs. D— I'm sorry." Anthony grimaced. "Should I call you Savannah?"

"Savannah is perfect," she said. "Now, what did you want to talk to me about?"

"If I could, I'd like to come out to your house and talk with you a bit," Anthony ventured.

Savannah sighed. "Is that truly necessary?"

"I think it is," Anthony insisted. "This investigation is stalled, and I have a sense I might be able to jump-start it if you and I talk."

"I don't know what it is you think I can tell you that's going to help you in this quest," Savannah said. "But, sure, if you want to come out here and talk to me, that's fine."

Anthony was a little surprised. He had thought she would refuse, and he'd carefully planned a speech to persuade her. Now it seemed his persuasive powers were unnecessary. "Thank you very much, Savannah," Anthony said. "When would be a good time for me to come out?"

"Whenever," she said dismissively. "It's not really a question of when's a good time. It's really a matter of which time is less bad." She paused for a moment. "Can you come this afternoon?" she asked.

"Yes." Anthony glanced at his calendar and noted a couple of other appointments he would have to cancel. "Yes, I can. Two o'clock?"

"Two o'clock will be fine. I'll see you then." Savannah hung up the phone.

Anthony immediately started making the calls he would need to make to clear his calendar for this new afternoon appointment. He didn't stop to think about why this appointment took precedence over the others—it just felt like the right thing to do.

Five

At two o'clock promptly, Anthony stood on the stoop of the Daileys' English Tudor home. As he listened to the door chime ring throughout the house, he again planned what he would say to coax information out of Savannah. When the door opened, before the chimes had completed their cycle, Anthony was struck by how drawn and pained Savannah looked.

"Hi," he said. "It's nice to see you again."

Savannah shrugged her shoulders. "Oh, I doubt that," she said. She held the screen door open for him to enter. "Come on in, let's get this over with."

Anthony followed her into the living-room, noticing how worn and tired she seemed. Although it was unprofessional of him and totally outside the realm of his responsibilities, he couldn't help asking, "Savannah, are you okay?"

"It's been a very difficult two weeks," Savannah said quietly, in what was most likely a huge understatement. "I've had a lot to deal with. You would think by now it would be getting easier, but it's not. I can't quite get used to the sad, pitying looks people give me." Savannah sat heavily on the sofa and motioned for him to sit on a nearby chair. "Seems everywhere I go, people know what happened. The girl at the grocery store, the teachers at the kids' school, even the counterman at the Chinese restaurant all seem to know that I have been abandoned by my husband. And they all tilt their heads sympathetically, and speak in soft tones to me as if they're afraid I might break at any moment. Frankly, it's getting very old."

"I can imagine," Anthony said.

"If I had my way, I would choose to act like none of this had ever happened. I would just go on, live my life, raise my children, and hang out with my sisters. And that's why, Mr. Martin"—she fixed a stern look at him—"I am not the least bit enthusiastic about having this conversation with you. Because talking to you about Dwayne makes it impossible for me to continue to live in my little fantasy that he didn't run off and leave us—he just *died*." She stopped short at the sound of that word. "That makes me kinda sick, doesn't it? I would rather my husband have died than have abandoned us. What kind of person does that make me?"

"An honest person," Anthony answered. "That's a completely honest, completely understandable reaction. You shouldn't be ashamed of yourself. And I do understand where you're coming from, but quite truthfully, Savannah, I believe you'll be able to get your life back to some normalcy sooner once you know what really happened."

"I'm not sure I believe that, Mr. Martin," she said. "But everybody else around me seems to, so I'm willing to accept that they might know something that I don't. In any event, you didn't come all the way out here to play psychiatrist and delve into my inner thoughts." She leaned forward and rested her elbows on her knees. "What is it you think I can do that will help?"

Anthony found himself once again admiring Savannah's see-it-through attitude. This was going to be a task that she did not relish, and he knew that. And the fact that she was willing to face it head-on said a lot to him about the type of woman Savannah Dailey was.

"I just have a couple of questions about your husband's activities immediately prior to his disappearance."

"Fire away, Mr. Martin," Savannah said.

Anthony made a face. "There's a little too much formality between us," he said. "I would really appreciate it if you would call me Anthony."

"Anthony, huh? Not Tony?"

Anthony smiled slightly. "My mother's side of my family all insists on calling me Antonio." He said the name with a slight Italian accent. "My father's side all insist on calling me Tony. I have always preferred Anthony, but it never seemed to matter to any of them." In the back of his mind, he wondered why he was telling her this. *What is it about Savannah Dailey that has me revealing intimate details about my family life?*

"I'm sorry," he said to her. "That was probably more than you wanted to know."

"No, it's okay," Savannah assured him. "So why Antonio?" Her curiosity was piqued.

"I think it's probably the Italian form of Anthony, and my mother's family holds on to their Italian heritage with a vengeance."

"I admire that," she said. "People have to have a culture that's important to them."

"Yes, I suppose so." Anthony nodded.

"And Tony?" she questioned.

"Well, that's my father's side of the family. Apparently, Anthony is too big a mouthful for them. They prefer Tony . . . some of them even just call me Tone."

"Tone?" Savannah laughed. "You don't strike me as a Tone."

Anthony shrugged. "I never felt like one. But I love my father's family, and if they want to call me Tone, I will certainly answer."

"Well, I'm going to call you Anthony, since you said that's your preference. But I've got to say, 'Tone' has a certain appeal to me."

"You, Savannah, may call me whatever you like," he said, surprising himself with his forwardness.

Savannah smiled and relaxed. This smiling, peaceful Savannah was a persona Anthony had never seen before. He couldn't help but notice how pretty she seemed when she was relaxed. Savannah was a mature beauty, thirty-eight, he knew from his research, but she wore her age gracefully, seeming completely comfortable with this age in her life. Her shoes caught Anthony's attention. She wore white leather Keds, the blue label at the back of the heel slightly worn, indicating that these shoes probably saw a lot of use. She was dressed in black capri pants and a peach-colored sleeveless sweater. She looked thinner than the last time he'd seen her—a change that could surely be attributed to the increased stress in her life. There were slight circles under her eyes that had not been there before, indicating that she probably was not sleeping well.

Forcing the less than professional thoughts from

his mind, Anthony turned his attention to the task at hand.

"What can you tell me about where your husband went, or who he saw, or what he did immediately preceding his disappearance?"

Savannah furrowed her brow, pushed a wayward piece of hair out of her eyes, and started to try to remember.

After an hour of picking her brain, Anthony had little more to go on. Dwayne for all intents and purposes had led a completely normal, completely average life—right up until the time he disappeared. Savannah had noted that he had been working very long hours—"or so he said," she added as an aside.

"We had a contract with a commercial builder that was severely taxing our resources since Dailey Plumbing is a small operation," she remembered. "Dwayne was working extra hours to try to fill the order. It was unusual but not out of character, given the job," she insisted.

Anthony scribbled notes on his pad and made a mental note to check with the builder to see if he'd been pleased with the work he'd received from Dailey Plumbing.

"That's all I can think of," Savannah said finally.

"You've done fine," Anthony encouraged her. "You've given me a couple of other things I can check out now."

"I'm curious," Savannah said, "why do you think it's taking so long to find him?"

"Well." Anthony shrugged. "Finding somebody who doesn't want to be found is not an easy task. This is someone who is actively hiding, and people like that can be very crafty."

Savannah nodded. "Actively hiding, huh? Well, I just feel special all over." She hugged her knees to her chest and looked away from him.

Anthony felt a need to reassure her. "It really doesn't have anything to do with you," he said. "Whatever drove your husband to this action didn't have anything to do with you, I'm sure of it. This is all about him."

"My sisters keep telling me that, too," she mumbled. "I don't see how that's possible. I was . . . am . . . his wife. He is obviously trying to get away from me."

"Savannah, I won't pretend to know anything about your marriage," Anthony began, "but I do know that what your husband did is a cowardly, illegal way to get out of a marriage that's not working. Millions of people end marriages every year with some dignity and consideration for the love they once had. This . . . this"—Anthony struggled not to say the curse word that pounded in his mind—*"man* chose to do something that would cause the maximum pain and humiliation. That says so much more about who he is than it does about you or your marriage."

Savannah lifted her head and smiled gratefully at him. "Thank you for that."

Anthony felt unexpectedly warmed by her smile. He was silent for a moment, enjoying the glow. "Well, I've taken up enough of your time," he said as he stood to leave. "Thank you again for agreeing to meet with me."

Savannah stood with him. "Well, sure, but I don't know how much help I was. I'd say you helped me a lot more than I helped you. Thank you for being so gracious and compassionate."

Anthony handed her his card. "Call me if you think of anything else, or if there's anything I can do for you."

"I will call you." She accepted the card. "And will you keep in touch?"

"I will most definitely keep in touch," Anthony assured her. They were shaking hands when her front door opened and D.J. and Stephanie came home from school.

"Hi, guys." Savannah dropped Anthony's hand and hugged each of her children. "How was school?"

"Same as always," D.J. said shortly.

Stephanie gave her brother a dirty look. "School sucks," she said as she threw her book bag in a corner.

"Why?" Surprise sprang onto Savannah's face. "What's going on?"

"Everybody keeps talking about Daddy and what happened." Stephanie's annoyance was obvious. She turned to Anthony. "You're that detective they hired, aren't you?"

"Yes, I'm Anthony Martin." He extended his hand to the girl. "Pleased to meet you. You're Stephanie, right?"

"Yes," she said, shaking his hand. "Everybody at school keeps joking about how Dad ran out on us. But I don't think it's funny."

"No," Anthony said slowly, "I don't imagine you would. And you're right, it isn't funny, but kids can be cruel."

"He's dead, isn't he?" D.J. asked. "That's the only

explanation. Otherwise he would have called me. Dad wouldn't just leave me like that. So he has to be dead, right?"

"D.J.," Savannah said wearily.

Stephanie looked expectantly at Anthony. "Is my daddy dead? Is that what you've come here to tell us? That my daddy's dead?"

"No, no." Anthony was quick to correct her. "That's not why I'm here at all. I came to find out some more information about your dad because I'm still looking for him. I don't believe he's dead."

"Are you sure?" Stephanie's tone was hopeful.

"Well, I can't be sure," Anthony admitted, "but none of the evidence I've turned up so far seems to suggest that your dad is dead." He turned to D.J. "I know this has been very difficult for you," he said, "trying to understand what's going on with your father. But I'm going to find him so that you can ask him yourself why he's done this thing. You're owed an explanation, and nobody but your father can give it to you."

D.J. nodded. "I just don't know what to think," he said quietly.

"I know," Anthony said. "And you shouldn't have to figure this out alone."

"You're sure he's not dead?" Stephanie said again.

"No, I'm not sure," Anthony said as gently as he could. "But I'm fairly certain that death is not what's keeping your father from you."

Stephanie's eyes teared up. "I don't know if that's a good thing or a bad thing."

Savannah hugged her daughter. "None of us do,

baby. None of us do." After a few moments, Savannah released Stephanie.

"Guys," she addressed the kids, "if you would excuse us, Mr. Martin and I have some business to finish up."

"Yes, ma'am," D.J. grunted and left the room without acknowledging Anthony.

Stephanie turned to follow her brother and then paused. "Please find my daddy," she said to Anthony. "I'm afraid he's in some kind of trouble."

"I promise I will," Anthony assured her, even though he usually made it a practice not to make any promises in business.

"I'm sorry if they were rude," Savannah said once the kids were gone.

"No, don't apologize. They weren't rude at all. They're just worried about their father." Anthony shook his head in disgust. "He didn't just run out on you, Savannah."

"I know . . . thank you for caring about my kids." Savannah laid a hand on his arm. "You didn't have to take that time to explain things to them. It means a lot to me that you did."

"I'm going to find him . . . you and your kids will have answers." Anthony felt his resolve strengthen. "I don't care how long it takes."

Savannah sensed his compassion and conviction. She felt more secure and protected than she had in a long time, including before Dwayne left. "Thank you" was all she could manage to say.

Six

After Anthony left, Savannah and the kids settled into their evening routine. Savannah noticed that the evening seemed to go more smoothly than had become normal for them since Dwayne's disappearance. She felt a renewed gratitude to Anthony Martin for his sensitivity.

The unexpected chime of the doorbell startled Savannah, interrupting her after dinner cleanup.

"Who could that be at this time of night?" Savannah muttered. She turned off the dishwater she was running in the sink and went to answer the door, hoping against hope that whoever it was, it would be something she could handle quickly and then close herself back up in her house.

"Yes?" She opened the door. Savannah's eyes widened in shocked and pleased astonishment.

"Jakarta!" she screamed. She rushed out of the door and buried her baby sister in a bear hug. "Jakarta, what are you doing here? When did you get here?"

Jakarta, thrilled to be in her sister's embrace, returned the hug with equal enthusiasm. "I came as soon as I heard, Savannah. I'm so sorry."

Savannah abruptly released her sister. "So Paris found you, I assume."

"Yes," Jakarta said. "When she told me what happened, I came home right away. How are you doing?"

"Oh, I don't know, Jakarta." Savannah suddenly sounded very weary. "I don't know how I'm doing. I just know this is the most difficult thing I've ever had to deal with." A slight smile brightened Savannah's face. "The one thing I do know is that I'm really glad to have my sisters around me, helping me get through this."

"Where else would we be?" Jakarta said.

Savannah pulled her sister into the house and closed the door. "How long can you stay, J?" she asked.

"As long as you need me to," Jakarta answered. "Assuming there's room here at Casa de Dailey for one homeless sister."

"Oh, of course you can stay here. I insist," Savannah said quickly. "But now how is it possible that you're able to stay here indefinitely? And what do you mean by 'homeless sister'? Does this mean that you don't have a job or a house or a boyfriend somewhere that you need to get back to?" Savannah eyed her baby sister with motherly concern.

"My priority is my family at this time," Jakarta said. "Nothing else really matters."

"Uh-huh," Savannah said, unconvinced. "I'll take that as a no. Where have you been, J?"

Jakarta shook her head. "This is not the time for me to talk about my travels. This is the time for us to focus on you."

"Uh-huh," Savannah repeated. "Okay, just tell me this. You haven't been doing anything illegal, have you?"

Jakarta gave a wry smile. "Define illegal."

"Jakarta!"

"Relax, big sister. I haven't been doing anything that you need to be worried about. What we need to be worried about is finding Dwayne." Jakarta deftly changed the subject. "By the way, where are the kids?" Jakarta looked around. "I want to give them a hug."

"They've gone to bed. They've been having a hard time dealing with all this," Savannah said. "Let's let them sleep . . . you'll see them tomorrow."

Jakarta nodded her head in agreement. "Okay, so tell me what's going on."

Savannah sighed. "J, I don't even know where to begin. Let's go to my room so we can talk."

As Savannah recounted recent events, she felt the sense of protection and security Anthony had left in his wake start to dissipate. Telling her youngest sister about her husband's betrayal seemed to leech the strength out of her spirit.

"So that's it," Savannah finished her story, "kicked in the teeth by the man I trusted more than anyone in the world. Pretty pathetic, huh?"

Jakarta grabbed her oldest sister's hands and pulled her in front of the mirror. "Savannah, look here. What do you see?"

Head bowed, shoulders slumped, Savannah stood in front of the full-length mirror that hung on the inside of the bedroom door.

"Look, Savannah," Jakarta demanded. Slowly, Savannah lifted her head.

"I see an abandoned wife," Savannah said as she turned to move away from the mirror.

"No." Jakarta held her firm. "Look again. Let me

tell you what I see." Jakarta stood behind Savannah and held her sister's upper arms, forcing her to face their images in the reflective glass. Jakarta stood a head shorter than Savannah, but the older woman's slumped posture made the sisters seem almost the same height. "Savannah, I see a strong, proud woman who has always been the bedrock of her family. And I don't just mean the Dailey family that lives in this house. I mean our whole Raven clan. My earliest memories are of you taking care of me. You know better than anybody I've been some pretty wild places and done some pretty outrageous things through the years. But I have always known that no matter where I was or what I was doing, I could always come home . . . to you . . . and be taken care of." Jakarta's eyes bored into Savannah's in the mirror. "Savannah, you will get through this. You will hold your family and your business together."

"It's too much, Jakarta. I can't do it alone." Savannah's voice was muffled. "Dwayne was always the one who took care of things. Hell, I must have been living in a cave or something." She shook free of her sister's hold and turned to face her. "I mean, how could I not know what he was planning? How does a man pack all his clothes, take all the money out of the bank and disappear, and his wife not know a thing? That detective Sydney hired must think I'm the biggest idiot in the world and he's probably right."

"First off, who cares what that detective thinks? He's being paid to do a job and he'll do it—regardless of what he thinks." Jakarta's expression grew hard.

"I care what he thinks," Savannah said. "I mean I

care what people think about me and this situation. Part of what makes this whole situation so hard to deal with is having people think I'm some kind of deaf, dumb, and blind fool."

"Savannah, on those many times when I came to you with my heart broken because some boy had cheated on me you used to tell me that if a person sets out to deceive you, you will be deceived. Don't you remember that?"

Savannah snorted and looked away.

"It was true then for me and my teenaged heart, and it's just as true now for you." Jakarta forced Savannah to meet her eyes. "You didn't know what Dwayne was up to because you trusted him . . . and because he didn't want you to know. He deceived and betrayed you, but that doesn't make you deaf, dumb, or blind. It makes you a woman who believed in her husband."

Savannah was quiet in the face of her baby sister's wisdom. "It's all just so hard, J. This was not supposed to happen to me. I built my life around this marriage, this family. Being a wife and mother is who and what I am."

"Savannah, that's not true," Jakarta protested.

"Yes, Jakarta, it is." Savannah walked to the window of her bedroom and gazed outside at the yard and Dwayne's workshop. "Everything about my life centered on my marriage. Look at my career choice. I was a communications major . . . I was going to go into broadcasting. I didn't go to school to learn how to run a plumbing business. Until I got married, and then Dwayne's dream became my dream. I never wanted to live way out here in the suburbs . . . I wanted to be closer to town, closer to the family, but

Dwayne thought this was the best neighborhood befitting his status. He picked the cars, the furniture, everything."

Savannah swung her head around to face her sister, causing her hair to swing in the breeze. "Hell, I even bought this hair because Dwayne liked women with long, flowing hair. So I got a weave to make my husband happy. How pathetic am I?"

"You're being too hard on yourself, sis," Jakarta said tenderly. "But if you're ready to reclaim your individuality, I know one thing that might help."

"What?" Savannah's curiosity was piqued.

"One of my many skills is doing hair. I can take that weave out so you can wear your hair however you want to," Jakarta offered.

"Really? Where did you learn to do hair?"

"Oh, you know," Jakarta hedged, "when you're out there in the world, you pick up all kinds of skills to survive."

"One day, Jakarta, we're going to sit down and you're going to tell me all about this life you've been leading since you left home." Savannah looked stern.

"Maybe, but not today," Jakarta said. "Today, we're going to do your hair. You game?"

"Yes," Savannah decided quickly. "Let's do it."

Giggling, the sisters went into Savannah's bathroom to begin.

Seven

The next morning, Savannah was in the kitchen finishing her second cup of coffee when Jakarta stumbled in.

"Good morning, Sleeping Beauty," Savannah said cheerfully. "I was afraid I wouldn't get a chance to see you before I left this morning."

"Coffee," Jakarta muttered. "Coffee first, conversation later." She headed to the cabinet, pulled out a mug, and poured a steaming cup of the dark, rich brew.

"I have to say it again, Jakarta, I love my hair!" Savannah's enthusiasm couldn't wait until her sister had consumed the coffee.

During their makeover session, Jakarta had removed all of the artificial hair from Savannah's head. Savannah's natural hair was damaged in some places, so Jakarta had recommended a haircut. The cut Savannah insisted on was dramatically shorter than Jakarta had envisioned.

"You were right about the hair, Savannah," Jakarta said after her second gulp of coffee. "I would never have imagined it, but that short Afro looks really good on you."

"I do look really good," Savannah decided. She patted her hair, enjoying the dramatic difference in texture between her natural hair and the weave she'd worn before. "You did a great job, J."

"You look so much better with your hair like this. I can't believe you spent all that time wearing a weave."

Savannah shook her head sadly. "The things we do for love."

Jakarta laughed. "Say that, sis. Say that."

The sisters shared a moment of understanding that women everywhere have experienced at one time or another in their lives.

"So where are my niece and nephew?" Jakarta asked. "I still haven't seen them yet."

"Well, they were in bed when you got here last night, and you were in bed when they left for school this morning," Savannah pointed out. "But they are both dying to see their cool Aunt Jakarta."

"I can't wait to see them, too." Jakarta smiled. "So what did they say about your hair?"

"Stephanie is a teenaged girl, and she thinks all women should have long hair. So the idea that I have voluntarily gotten rid of long hair has just freaked her out." Savannah grinned. "She said she likes my Afro okay, but she simply cannot understand why I wouldn't want to have long, flowing hair."

"It's because of those music videos," Jakarta declared. "They've completely skewed kids' views. Kids watch those things all day long and that's where their image of beautiful comes from."

"Maybe." Savannah nodded. "D.J., however, didn't say anything. D.J. hasn't had much of anything to say ever since his dad disappeared. It's been so hard for him."

"It hasn't been any harder on him than it has been for the rest of you," Jakarta said.

"I actually think it has been," Savannah disagreed. "The relationship between a boy and his father is not something either one of us can understand—not being boys—but D.J. feels particularly betrayed by his father. He seems to keep hoping that something will turn up that will somehow prove this situation is not what it appears to be."

Jakarta shook her head sadly. "What can we do?"

"All we can do is be here for him. Make sure he knows he's loved," Savannah said. "Okay, enough of that." Savannah abruptly changed the subject. "What are you going to do today?"

"Well, I don't have any plans. I thought I'd hang out here and do whatever I could to help you out," Jakarta replied.

"Did you plan to contact your sisters?" Savannah studied Jakarta closely.

"Well, I hadn't thought about it," Jakarta said slowly, "but I guess I will."

"Uh-huh. Make sure you call your sisters," Savannah insisted. "I would have called them for you, but I thought that might be something you'd want to do yourself."

"Why are you making so big a deal out of it?" Jakarta asked. "I've just come home for an extended visit."

"Oh, please." Savannah gave her baby sister a stern look. "It is a big deal, and you know it. And Sydney and Paris are going to want to see you and spend time with you, so you need to just go on and make the call."

"Yes, ma'am," Jakarta said mockingly.

"As a matter of fact, why don't you call Paris now?" Savannah got up from her chair and retrieved the cordless phone from its base on the wall. "Sydney is probably already on her way to work, but you might still be able to catch Paris." She placed the phone on the table in front of Jakarta.

Jakarta sighed. "You're making a bigger deal out of this than it is."

"Seems like you're the one making the bigger deal out of it, refusing to make the call." Savannah folded her arms across her chest. "Go on and call your sister."

"Okay, okay, I'll call my sister," Jakarta huffed. She snatched the phone off the table and dialed Paris's number. Savannah watched silently as Jakarta listened for an answer.

"She must be gone already," Jakarta said after a pause. "There's no answer."

"Just hold on," Savannah insisted, "her machine will pick up in a minute."

Jakarta rolled her eyes at her sister, but held on as she had been instructed. Shortly, Paris's voice mail picked up.

"Hey, Paris, it's Jakarta," Jakarta said into the machine. "I'm here in town at Savannah's. Call me when you get this message." She hung up the phone. "Happy now?" She turned to Savannah.

"Ecstatic," Savannah said. "Now if you will excuse me, I have to go to work."

"Work?" Jakarta's brow furrowed in question.

"Hey, somebody's gotta run Dailey Plumbing." Savannah shrugged. "Guess it's gotta be me."

"What do you know about running a plumbing business?"

"Dwayne and I have had this business for eleven years. I know one or two things."

"Well, I'm sure you're not completely ignorant about the business, but—"

"Look, Jakarta," Savannah cut her off, "I have to do this. I will not let my business fall apart. Now if you want to be helpful around here, you can make sure dinner is ready for us this evening."

"Oh, so now I'm the cook," Jakarta said playfully.

"Chief cook and bottle washer," Savannah teased. "Hey, you said you wanted to help."

"Okay, okay," Jakarta agreed. "Have a good day, boss lady."

Savannah nodded and grabbed her coat off a hook near the door. She climbed into her car and headed for Dailey Plumbing. In the cocoon of her sisters' support, Savannah was slowly beginning to come to terms with her new life. She had grabbed the reins of the company and was pleased to find she had a natural aptitude for business. At first, the employees were resistant and resentful. The bad taste the bounced checks had created had not fully left them, but gradually Savannah was able to win them over.

And now she would have to face one of the most difficult days she'd experienced ever since she took over the business. She'd been over the books backward and forward, sat with the company accountant and with her sister Sydney, trying to figure a way to avoid what she had to do today. But she could see no way out.

The business just cannot support this number of employees. She sighed. *I have to let some of them go in order to save the business for the others.*

"The needs of the many outweigh the needs of the few," she said aloud, trying to draw strength from the sound of the words in her ears and make her peace with this decision. But it wasn't becoming any easier to her.

As she drove to the shop, Savannah mentally went through the list of employees, weighing the pros and cons, considering each person's situation, trying to decide who could stay and who would have to go.

It's killing me to have to make these kinds of decisions about these men's futures. But there really is no other way.

By the time she'd parked her car in the Dailey Plumbing lot, she was fairly confident about her decision. *Six people have to go,* she decided. *I hope it will only be temporary, but I have to lay off six of the men.*

When she entered the shop, she was greeted by some of the workers.

"Hey, Mrs. Dailey!"

"Morning Mrs. D!"

She smiled and waved at each of them. Once she got to the office that had been Dwayne's that she had now claimed for herself, she pulled out the list of employees who were scheduled to be laid off. She reviewed the list one more time to make sure this was the best of a bad choice.

"There is no other way," she told herself again. "There just isn't." Resolve in place, she went out into the shop and asked each of the six men to come to her office.

"Gentlemen," she said once they were all assembled, "there is no easy way for me to do this. I've been over the books a hundred times, and there is simply no alternative."

The men were quiet, apparently anticipating what was to come.

"As you all know," Savannah continued, "Dailey Plumbing has been experiencing some very difficult times ever since Mr. Dailey left." The men nodded, but still stood silently. "Because of those difficult times, I'm going to have to make a move I never thought I'd make. I'm going to have to lay you off."

The men's reactions were varied.

"No! You can't do that."

"I have a family to support."

"Mrs. Dailey, please, can't you do something else?"

Two of the older men stood stoically, not showing any emotion. Two of the other men shook their heads sadly. And two of the men responded angrily.

"How could you do this to me? I've been with this company for five years. Doesn't that count for something?"

"Kent," Savannah said slowly, "loyalty counts for everything. Loyalty is the reason why I've put off layoff for this long. I tried to find a way to avoid it. I did everything I could, but it couldn't be avoided. Dailey Plumbing simply cannot afford a full workforce right now."

"Well, why should we all have to suffer because Mr. Dailey was a damn dog?" another man demanded.

"Dante." Savannah met his eyes. "I wish I had the answer to that. You don't know how many times I've asked myself that exact question since this whole ordeal began. I wish I could say something that would make this easier for you, but I know I can't." Savannah stepped back so she could see each of them.

"All I can tell each of you is that as soon as we're back on our feet, as soon as Dailey Plumbing's economic picture improves, I will hire you all back. You each have been instrumental in building Dailey Plumbing. I want to thank you for your patience, your understanding, and your support. And I promise, I will hire you back just as soon as I can."

"Promises from a Dailey, huh?" Kent sneered. "I can't think of anything that's worth less."

"Look, man, no point coming down on her," one of the other employees said. "That snake Dwayne Dailey is who we should go after. No offense, Mrs. Dailey," he added. "You do what you have to do to take care of your business."

"Thank you, Walter." Savannah nodded gratefully. "This layoff won't be any longer than it has to be." She crossed the room and retrieved six envelopes from her desk drawer. "I have prepared severance checks for each of you. You can, of course, apply for unemployment. And I will understand if you have to get another job before I'm able to hire you back."

"Oh, you will, will you?" Dante said. "Well, ain't that nice of you!"

Walter gave the younger man a look that silenced him.

"I don't know what else I can say at this point," Savannah said. "Thank you and keep in touch."

"Whatever," Dante said shortly.

After the men filed out of her office, Savannah collapsed into the plush leather chair Dwayne had ordered. "That was so much harder than I thought it was going to be," she said. "I've got to get those men back here. I owe them that." She reached for her company ledger book and turned to the accounts receivable page. She scrolled down the list of clients who owed the company.

Customers were another huge area of concern for Savannah. When Dwayne disappeared, the news had spread very quickly through the community. Dailey Plumbing's customers were equally quick to voice concerns about Savannah's ability to maintain the business.

It had taken much cajoling, groveling, and bargaining on her part to convince the customers not to pull their business. She had not been completely successful. Some of the bigger accounts had been simply unwilling to take the chance on her. Some had left apologetically and some had left angrily, but almost half of the Dailey Plumbing customer base had fled. Savannah had had to agree to extraordinary deals and deep discounts to get the others to stay.

Now, as she scanned the list of past due accounts, she recognized several of the departed customers. *I'm not looking forward to talking to these people again,* she thought. *The last time was unpleasant enough.*

She mulled it over for a few moments and then gathered her resolve and decided to start calling in the debts.

"The sooner I can get these bills paid, the sooner I can get Dailey Plumbing back on its feet."

Anthony Martin sat at his desk, equally consumed with the business of Dailey Plumbing, but for a different reason. After having talked to several of the Daileys' customers, he was surprised to discover that their business had an excellent reputation and was well regarded by their customers. Because of Dwayne's actions, Anthony fully expected to find a man trying to escape from a failing business. However, the contrary was true.

This makes less and less sense, Anthony thought. *Why would this man, who apparently was doing well in business and had a loving family, leave like that?*

Understanding why Dwayne left was not really necessary to figure out where Dwayne went. It wasn't really a part of the job Anthony needed to do. But he found himself fascinated by Dwayne Dailey and his really bad decisions. Thoughts of Dwayne inevitably led Anthony to thoughts of Savannah.

I wonder how she's holding up?

He considered calling her, but decided against it. *I don't have any news for her,* he realized. *There's no reason to call her and get her hopes up just because I want to see how she's doing.*

The realization of the logic of those words did not make it any easier for Anthony to avoid making the call anyway. Anthony was pondering his options when a knock at his office door interrupted his thoughts.

"Come in," he called automatically, not looking up.

"Um, hello, Mr. Martin. I hope I'm not disturbing you." Savannah peeked tentatively around the door.

Anthony sat up, immediately at attention. "Savannah," he said. "I wasn't expecting you." He rose from his desk and crossed the room to usher her in. "Please, come in and have a seat." As he watched her settle into the chair, he noticed her new look. "Wow," he said. "Your hair looks great." Then, suddenly, he realized the inappropriateness of his words. "I'm sorry, Savannah. I shouldn't have said that."

"Why?" Savannah looked puzzled. "You don't really like my hair?"

Anthony shook his head vigorously. "No, I really do like your hair . . . but you are a client and this is a professional business office. I should not be commenting on anything as personal as your hairstyle. I apologize."

Savannah laughed. "Mr. Martin, it is never inappropriate to compliment a lady on her looks. Even in a professional business office."

"Well, in that case." Anthony smiled. "Your hair looks fabulous. When did you get it done?"

"I got it done last night, as a matter of fact." Savannah patted her hair. "My baby sister, Jakarta, came home last night, and she did it for me."

Anthony shook his head. "Another sister? Let me see if I've got this right—Savannah, Sydney, Paris, and now Jakarta? Got any other sisters? Or any brothers—Rome or Madrid maybe?"

"Nope," Savannah said, laughing, "just the four of us girls."

"And what's up with the city names?" Anthony asked.

"I've never really known," Savannah admitted. "I guess Mom and Dad just thought it would be cute. Believe me, these names have gotten us quite a bit of attention, especially when we were kids. They certainly made the Raven sisters memorable."

"It is not only your name that makes you memorable." The words slid from Anthony's mind to his lips before he could stop them. *Oh, Lord—what did I just say?* Embarrassed, Anthony busied himself by taking his seat and putting a case file in the center of his desk. "Uh, you never did say . . . what can I do for you?"

Savannah watched his nervous movements with slight amusement. "Nothing really," she said. "I just wanted to stop by and thank you again for being so considerate with my children. It meant a lot to them and it meant a lot to me, too."

Anthony nodded. "You are certainly welcome, Savannah. They are great kids, and anything I can do to help, I'm willing to."

"That's good to know, Mr. Martin," she said.

He made a face at her. "I thought we had agreed that you were going to call me Anthony," he insisted.

"Well, actually, I was still considering 'Tone.'" Her smile could be heard in the words.

Anthony groaned with mock dismay. "No, no— not another 'Tone' fan."

"You have to admit, it does have a certain style." She laughed. "In any event, Anthony, I won't keep you from your day. I just wanted to take a moment to thank you again." She rose from the chair to leave.

Inexplicably unready to let her leave, Anthony quickly wracked his brain for a reason to make her stay.

"Hold on . . . this is not fair," Anthony protested.

Savannah looked confused. "What's not fair?"

"You know all my nicknames—you've even threatened to call me Tone. But I don't know any nickname for you." He smiled and leaned closer to her across the desk. "'Savannah' seems like it would have been a mouthful for kids when you were younger. Anybody ever call you anything else?"

Savannah paused for a moment, apparently considering the question. "I probably shouldn't tell you this," she said finally. "How do I know you won't use it against me some day?"

Anthony held up his hand as if taking an oath. "Scout's honor; I'll keep it just between us."

Savannah pretended to scrutinize him. "Well, I guess you look trustworthy enough," she decided. "When I was a kid, my dad used to call me Pokey." She made a face as she said the name.

"Pokey?" Anthony struggled to control his laughter. "Why?"

"Sydney and I used to be inseparable, and we were always getting into trouble. Daddy used to call us Gumby and Pokey—you know, after the cartoon characters." Savannah shook her head at the memory. "I never really understood why Sydney got to be Gumby and I had to be Pokey," Savannah said. "Probably because she was the ringleader, always cooking up the trouble."

"So you and Sydney used to be inseparable?" Anthony asked. "You said that with a little melancholy."

"Oh, you don't really want to hear all this," Savannah said.

"Really I do," he assured her. "It sounds like it might be an interesting story." He gestured to the chair she had vacated. "Please tell me about it."

"Okay," Savannah warned as she sat back down. "You asked for it."

"Duly warned." He smiled. "Now tell me about you and your sisters."

"We grew up very close, but then as we got to be adults, our interests took us in different directions. Sydney has always been focused on making money."

Anthony tilted his head at her. "You say she has

always been focused on making money like it's a bad thing."

"It's not necessarily a bad thing," Savannah allowed, "but when it becomes the single driving focus of your life—to the exclusion of everything and everybody else, including family—then it's a problem."

"And that's what you feel Sydney has done?"

"Don't get me wrong, I really admire Sydney's business savvy. She made a killing when the dot coms were hot, and she was smart enough to take her money and run before the bottom fell out." Savannah shrugged. "It's just that while Sydney was busy chasing that dollar, she was drifting further and further away from her family."

Anthony watched her quietly for a moment, waiting to see if she would go on.

"It's really kinda sad," she said finally. "When we were kids, Sydney and I were two halves of the same whole. We were closer to each other than we were with either Paris or Jakarta. But then we grew up and things changed."

Noticing her sadness, Anthony quickly changed the subject. "What about Paris? What does she do?"

"Paris is an elementary school teacher. She is very devoted to her students. She teaches the fourth grade, and they all love Ms. Raven. Most of her students come back even once they get to high school to visit Ms. Raven." Savannah smiled with pride. "Paris has always sort of been the peacemaker in the family. She's the one who has kept up with everybody and kept us all close—well, semiclose anyway," Savannah corrected.

"And tell me about this newest sister that I haven't

met yet," Anthony prompted. "Jakarta, did you say her name was?"

Savannah smiled broadly. "Jakarta is the baby of the family and she has always been our wild child. I guess because she was so much younger than the rest of us, she was always old for her age, always running after us trying to keep up. And now as an adult, she's usually off doing her own thing."

"You mentioned your dad earlier," Anthony reminded her. "Where are your parents?"

"Mom and Dad were killed by a drunk driver several years ago. It was a horrible thing." Savannah sat quietly, reflecting. "I think that's when we all started drifting apart. We could always count on being able to get together with Mom and Dad, at the holidays if no other time. But once that center was gone, it became easier and easier for all of us to go our own ways." Savannah sat back in the chair. "Paris does a good job of keeping in touch with everybody, at least letting us know what's going on in everybody else's life. We still get together now and again, but it's never been the same since Mom and Dad were killed."

Anthony nodded thoughtfully. "Well, I know I'm just on the outside looking in, but it seems to me that you and your sisters are very close. They certainly seem to be rallying to your side."

Savannah smiled slightly. "I guess if one good thing has come out of this whole ordeal with Dwayne it's that my sisters and I have reunited. For how long, I can't say, but I'm going to enjoy it while it lasts." Savannah placed her hands on the arms of the chair and pushed up. "Now I really have taken up enough of your time," she declared. "You have to get back to work, and so do I. Thank you again, Anthony, for your kindness and compassion. And thanks for letting me ramble on about my family."

"You're welcome, Savannah," he said earnestly. "I enjoyed talking with you. And really, anything I can do I will."

She said, "I guess I'll talk to you later."

"Yes, you will," he assured her. "I'll call you as soon as I find out anything about your missing husband."

"Oh, goody," she said dryly, "I can hardly wait." Savannah nodded her good-bye and eased out the door.

As he watched her leave, Anthony felt an almost paternal need to protect her—almost paternal. One of the things Anthony prided himself on was being honest with himself. It was a characteristic that helped in his business. So when he forced himself to deal honestly with his feelings for Savannah Dailey, he knew they were not all paternal . . . and not all professional.

Anthony realized anew that finding Dwayne was very low on Savannah's list of priorities. *He still needs to be found,* Anthony thought stubbornly. *He needs to be found and he needs to explain himself. I will not let this man get away with betraying his family.* Anthony reached again for the Dailey file and again began to pore over it.

Eight

When Savannah arrived home that evening, she was a little miffed to find Jakarta and the kids playing video games and no dinner prepared.

"Well, what have we here?" she said.

"Hey, sis. Hang on a second." Jakarta fiercely punched the buttons on the game controller and maneuvered her game character. D.J. and Stephanie whooped with laughter as Jakarta narrowly avoided being disintegrated.

"Ha!" she yelled. "I told you I was the queen of this game!"

"I can beat that score," D.J. declared.

"You wish!" Stephanie laughed.

"I'd like to see you try," Jakarta teased as she passed him the controller.

Savannah watched the scene with mixed emotions. While she was happy to see her sister and her children enjoying each other's company, she was annoyed that dinner was not ready, and apparently, no one seemed especially interested in preparing it.

"I thought we agreed that dinner was going to be your job," she said to her sister.

"Wait, hold on," Jakarta said defensively. "I was ready to cook, but then Paris called and she insisted that we come to her house for dinner."

"A meal to welcome the prodigal sister home, I assume?"

"Yeah, something like that." Jakarta grimaced. "We're supposed to be there at seven sharp."

"You need to quit acting like you're being led to a firing squad," Savannah said. "It's just sisters getting together for a meal."

Jakarta made a face. "I just hope the menu for the night is not 'rack of grilled Jakarta.' "

Savannah laughed as she draped her coat on the back of a chair. "Guess there's only one way to find out."

At seven, the Dailey family—Savannah, D.J., and Stephanie, with Jakarta in tow—converged on Paris's comfortable town house. Paris rushed out of the house, hurrying to hug her baby sister.

"I am so glad you came home," Paris said.

"I had to come, P," Jakarta replied. "Aside from the fact that you weren't hearing *no* excuses"—the sisters laughed—"I knew you were right. I knew I had to be here."

"Is Sydney here yet?" Savannah asked.

Paris turned to answer the question and noticed Savannah's hair for the first time.

"Oh, my gosh! Savannah! Your hair!" Paris released Jakarta and rushed over to pat Savannah's freshly cropped do. "When did you do this?"

"Jakarta did it for me last night. Do you like it?" Savannah asked anxiously.

"Like it?" Paris exclaimed. "I love it! It makes you look younger and thinner."

Savannah made a face. "Did I look old and fat before?"

"Oh, of course not." Paris shook her head. "You

just look so different with that haircut! Who knew hair could make that big a difference?"

"So, you never said," Jakarta reminded Paris, "is Sydney here yet or not?"

"No," Paris answered, "she called to say she was running late, but she would be here as soon as she could. And"—Paris hugged Jakarta again—"she said she's really excited about seeing you."

"I doubt very seriously that that's what she said," Jakarta said.

"Give her a chance," Paris insisted.

"Yeah," Savannah said, "Sydney has really come through for me during all this. More than I ever expected or gave her credit for."

"Okay." Jakarta shrugged. "You two know best."

"Come on in the kitchen," Paris said. "You can talk to me while I finish up."

The women retreated to the kitchen, while the kids settled in front of the TV. The sisters had been in Paris's kitchen finishing dinner for about forty minutes when Sydney arrived and breezed through the door.

"I cannot believe it," Sydney said. "They told me you were here, and I said, 'I have to see it for myself.' And look—here you are!"

Jakarta rose from her seat and crossed the room to hug her sister. "Hey, Syd! How ya doing?"

"How am I doing?" Sydney said. "That does not matter one iota. All that matters is that you're here."

Jakarta looked curiously at her, not sure whether or not Sydney was sincere in her welcome.

"Oh, stop being silly," Sydney said, noticing Jakarta's look. "Whatever else has happened between us, you are still my sister. And I'm thrilled to have you home." The two sisters embraced once more.

Over Jakarta's shoulder, Sydney got a look at Savannah's hair. "What have you done?" She abruptly released Jakarta and practically ran to Savannah's side. "Your hair! What have you done to your hair?"

Laughing, Savannah ran her fingers through the short Afro. "You sound like my daughter—horrified."

"Maybe not horrified," Sydney said, "but certainly surprised. Why . . . when . . . ?"

"It's okay, Syd." Savannah grinned. "Take a deep breath. I had Jakarta cut my hair last night. It was time for a change."

"That is most definitely a change," Sydney said. "Do you like it?"

"Yeah, I like it a lot. I take it you don't?" Savannah asked.

"It's . . . it's . . . it's different," Sydney managed. She stepped back and studied Savannah carefully. "It looks good on you," she said finally. "It flatters your bone structure."

"Whew!" Savannah teased. "That's a load off my mind."

"Okay, guys, dinner's ready," Paris said. She called the kids into her small dining room, and everyone took a seat around the table.

"D.J., would you ask the blessing?" Paris said to her nephew.

D.J. looked uncomfortably around the table. "I don't know, Aunt Paris. That was always Daddy's job."

"But your daddy's not here right now," Paris said

gently, "and I can't think of anybody else I would rather have fill his shoes."

D.J. relaxed and nodded. "Yes, ma'am," he said.

Savannah smiled gratefully at her sister.

"Would you all please bow your heads?" D.J. said. "Dear God, we ask your blessings upon this food and this family, and, God, please be with my daddy wherever he is and help him return safely to us. Amen."

"Amen," the women around the table intoned.

"That was a lovely prayer, D.J.," Savannah said.

"You think God will hear it?" D.J. asked.

Savannah nodded. "Of course God will hear it. God hears all prayers."

"Will he answer it?" D.J. persisted.

"God always answers our prayers," Paris interjected. "It's just that sometimes, the answer is 'No.'"

The table fell silent for a moment while each person processed those words.

"Okay, that's enough of those long faces," Jakarta said abruptly. "This is supposed to be a welcome-home party for me. So how come I ain't got none of that lasagna on my plate?"

The table erupted with laughter, and food platters and trays began to be passed around the table with earnest. The next two hours were spent in joyful family reunion, with laughter and talking filling the room. The Raven sisters sat at Paris's table giggling and enjoying themselves like the little girls they once were. For a while at least, there were no troubles—no wayward husbands, no wild and wasted youths, no pressing business matters, no concerns about calories and cholesterol. For a little while, they were little girls again.

Over dessert, Sydney brought them all back to the present.

"So what's the status of the investigation?" she asked. "I gave Anthony Martin permission to contact you . . . has he found anything out?"

Savannah sighed, not really wanting to get into *that* topic of conversation. "He came by," she said, "but he didn't have any news. He came by to see if there was anything else I knew."

Paris grinned wickedly as she poured coffee for her sisters. "That is one good-looking man."

Savannah sipped her coffee with studied indifference. "I hadn't really noticed. Is he handsome?"

Paris shot her a look that spoke volumes. "Oh, yeah, right, you didn't notice. You might be upset, but you are not blind. And he came by your house? Lucky girl. He is one fine piece of eye candy."

"Oh, is that right?" Jakarta said. "So when do I get to meet this detective?"

"Ladies, focus," Sydney said. "The man has a job to do for us. That's what we need to be talking about."

"I can't see any reason why we can't focus on both things." Paris giggled. "Can you, Jakarta?"

"Okay, that's enough," Savannah said. "To answer your question, Syd, there is no new information yet, but Mr. Martin has promised to keep us posted." She turned to Paris and Jakarta, whose faces were still lit with broad grins. "And as for you two, Anthony Martin is running an investigation, that's all he is to me."

"If you say so, Savannah." Paris sounded unconvinced. "If you say so."

Soon, the evening ended, and it was time for the sisters to depart and head back to their own lives.

"Are you sure you can't stay any longer?" Paris said to Savannah as she and the kids prepared to leave.

"Sorry, sis," Savannah said genuinely, "it's a school night and we've all got to get up in the morning."

"So how are you adjusting to running the business?" Sydney looked up from the glass of wine she was drinking to ask.

"Today was a really rough day," Savannah said. "I had to lay some of the guys off. It's so unfair. The guys at the shop have all been wonderful. They've been doing some extra work to try and get us out of this hole."

"And how soon do you think you're going to be out of the hole?" Sydney said.

"Worried about your money, Syd?" Savannah asked.

"Not worried," Sydney assured her, "just curious."

"I think it will be soon," Savannah said. "And just in case I haven't said it recently, thank you again for bailing us out."

Sydney nodded. "You know what, Savannah, I'm really glad I was in a position to be able to do it."

Savannah laughed. "So am I."

"So what are you doing now that you're in town, Jakarta?" Sydney turned to her youngest sister just as she was slipping on her coat.

"I knew it was too good to be true," Jakarta said. "I knew there was no way I was getting through a whole dinner with Sydney without talk of my future coming up."

"You act like it's a bad thing," Sydney said, "to be

worried about my baby sister and want the best for her."

"I appreciate your concern, Syd, really I do," Jakarta said. "But I don't know what I'm going to be doing yet. What I'm going to be doing in the short term is staying at Savannah's house and helping her out however I can."

"Okay," Sydney said. "But when you're ready to start looking for a job, let me know. I have some connections and I might be able to help."

Jakarta nodded gravely. "Yes, Sydney, I will." Jakarta turned to Savannah. "Okay, okay, you were right. Sydney has mellowed a bit. But she is still all up in everybody's business."

Sydney bristled at her words and prepared to defend herself.

"But, Jakarta." Savannah quickly diffused the situation. "You always have had the best business to be all up in."

Laughter met that comment, as Sydney relaxed and laughed as well. After kisses all around, Savannah, Jakarta, and the children headed home.

Nine

Everyone fell into a routine to get through the days. Savannah was handling the business with remarkable aplomb. Once the trauma of laying off the employees was behind her, she was able to focus on saving the business and getting it back on solid financial ground. D.J. and Stephanie were thrilled to have their Aunt Jakarta with them. The three of them began to do more and more together as Jakarta tried to fill the void left by their missing father.

The family got together on a weekly basis for dinner at one of their houses just to keep in touch. Paris had insisted that they do that, noting that it was far too easy to lose track of each other. Paris was determined not to let the family fall out of touch again.

Anthony tracked down lead after lead in his quest to find Dwayne. He was frustrated by his lack of progress.

"It's one step forward, two steps back," he said, annoyed. His voice filled his empty office as he yet again studied the Dailey file. "As soon as I find him someplace, he slips away." Anthony had developed the habit of making weekly reports to Sydney and Savannah of his progress. While Sydney was impatient, Savannah was serene.

"I'm sure you're doing the best you can," she

once said. "You told me that if somebody doesn't want to be found, it's hard to find him."

As Anthony remembered the conversation, he was grateful for her patience, but frustrated with his inability to locate Dwayne. The last place the paper trail of evidence showed Dwayne as being was Houston, Texas. Anthony had a call in to a fellow private detective in Houston who promised to check on the lead Anthony had given him. Anthony decided to call his Texas friend to see if there was any news.

"Hey, Manuel," Anthony said.

"Tony Martin, good to hear from you," Manuel replied.

"Do you have any news about my guy?" Anthony said without preamble.

"Actually, I do," Manuel said. "I was going to call you later today."

Anthony perked up. "What've you got?"

"Seems that Dwayne Dailey, also known as Kevin Edwards, is currently going by Randolph Mann. And he's in New Orleans."

"New Orleans now?" Anthony felt his frustration return.

"Guess your boy wants to see the world," Manuel said. "But the last record we have of him here in Houston was him boarding a plane for New Orleans."

"All right," Anthony said. "New Orleans it is. Thanks for your help, Manny." Anthony hung up the phone, immediately reached for his Rolodex, and spun through the names and numbers of other detectives he knew.

"New Orleans, New Orleans . . ." he mumbled under his breath as he flipped through the cards. He finally located a contact he had not used for quite some time. "Hopefully this is the last place I have to track him to," Anthony muttered. "I'll get on a plane and go to New Orleans and tie him down myself if I have to." Anthony made the call to his fellow detective.

"Jocelyn," he said once the line was answered. "This is Anthony Martin in Detroit."

"Anthony! What a nice surprise!" the female voice responded. "I haven't heard from you in forever it seems. What's going on?"

"Actually, Jocelyn, I've got a case I need you to help me with." Quickly, Anthony briefed her on the details of the Dailey investigation. "And now I hear he's in your town . . . I wonder if you might be able to track him down?"

"I'll do what I can for you," Jocelyn said. "What was that name again?"

Anthony repeated the pseudonym Dwayne was using.

"Okay, I'll let you know if I find anything."

"Thanks, Jocelyn. It's kinda important that we do this as quickly as possible. My boy's got a habit of moving around," Anthony warned.

"Say no more," Jocelyn said. "I'll get right on it."

After he hung up with Jocelyn, Anthony debated calling Savannah and telling her what was going on. But he decided against it, realizing that he really didn't have anything new to tell her. "Not yet," he said, "but soon."

At her desk at the office, Savannah, with the phone receiver cradled between her ear and her shoulder, was gently massaging the bridge of her nose, trying to stay calm.

"I know you're frustrated, Mr. Wright," she said. "And I do appreciate your patience with us. The plumbing supplies we need to do your job have simply not arrived yet. As soon as we get them, I'm sending a crew over to your job site to take care of it for you."

Savannah listened as her customer vented his anger. "I do understand," she assured him. "This should be handled by the end of the week. Thank you again for your patience. I'll call you if anything changes." She hung up the phone with a weary expression on her face. She rubbed her temples, trying to ease some of the stress away. Out of the corner of her eye, she caught a glimpse of the most recent report that Anthony had sent.

It's been almost eight months, Savannah thought, *and Dwayne is still on the run. Dwayne's out living the life, while I'm here arguing with customers and suppliers. Something is just not fair about that.*

She allowed herself a brief moment of anger at the situation, and then realized she had to press on. She looked down at the list of calls she had to make and picked up the phone to call the plumbing supplier next.

"I need to light a fire under him," she said with a steely glint in her eyes. "I have not come this far to let it all be ruined by a slow-moving supplier."

Anthony answered the phone on the first ring, hoping it was news from New Orleans.

"Anthony Martin, who's your best friend in the

world?" Jocelyn the detective in New Orleans asked playfully.

"You tell me, Joce," Anthony responded. "Are you about to make my day?"

"As a matter of fact, I am," she said. "I found your boy. He's registered at one of the hotels in the French Quarter. Been here for about a week from what I can tell."

Anthony made quick notes as she gave him the name and address of the hotel. "Is there anything else you can tell me?" he asked.

"Just that your boy is a big tipper and something of a party animal," Jocelyn replied.

"Why am I not surprised by that?" Anthony grumbled. "Thanks, Joce, for getting back to me so quickly."

"Hey, Martin, I'm good at what I do—this little favor was a piece of cake. Next time, give me something hard to do."

Anthony laughed. "I owe you one, Jocelyn."

"Oh, and believe me, Martin, I will be collecting," she said playfully. "Next time you're in New Orleans, look me up."

"That's a deal," Anthony said. "Thanks again, Jocelyn." He hung up the phone and immediately called the New Orleans hotel to make sure that Dwayne was still there before he went to Savannah with the information.

With flares of excited anticipation coursing through his blood, Anthony listened as the long-distance call was connected. When the hotel operator answered, he asked for the name Jocelyn had given him.

"One moment, sir, I'll connect you."

Anthony held his breath as the line rang.

"Hello?" a gruff male voice answered.

"Randolph Mann, please?" Anthony said.

"This is Randolph Mann; who's calling?" Suspicion laced the words.

"Um, Mr. Mann, this is the hotel manager," Anthony lied smoothly. "I was just calling to make sure that everything is satisfactory with your accommodations and the treatment you are receiving from the staff." Anthony had no intention of letting Dwayne know the truth—that his old life in Detroit had caught up with him.

"Oh, everything's fine." The man's voice relaxed. "It's good of you to check."

"You are one of our favorite guests, Mr. Mann," Anthony continued in his charade, "and your happiness is of paramount importance to us."

"Well, that's good to know. This is one class joint you've got here."

"Thank you, sir," Anthony replied. "Please don't hesitate to let me or my staff know if there is anything we can do to make your stay here more enjoyable."

"You bet I will," the man answered.

Anthony decided to risk one last question. "Will you be staying with us much longer, Mr. Mann?"

The phone line hummed quietly in the silence. "I haven't decided yet," the man said after a long pause. "I'll be here a few more days at least."

"Very good, sir," Anthony said quickly. "Have a nice day."

"Yeah, you, too." Randolph Mann né Dwayne Dailey hung up the phone.

Anthony was beside himself with excitement. He

jumped up from his desk, grabbed his coat from the rack near the door, and raced to his car, barely remembering to lock his office on the way out.

"I cannot wait to tell Savannah," he said. He covered the distance between his office and hers in record time. He took a chance that she would be at the plumbing shop. He hadn't called ahead, wanting to surprise her. When he arrived at Dailey Plumbing, he was relieved to recognize Savannah's car in the parking lot. He parked his car and practically ran into the building. He barely noticed the curious stares of Savannah's employees as he speed-walked through the shop, heading for her office in the back. After knocking one quick time, he flung open the door and burst in.

Ten

"Savannah, I found him." Anthony looked very pleased with himself. "I had to trace him to several different cities, and under several different names, but I found him in a hotel in New Orleans."

"New Orleans? What's he doing there?"

Anthony shrugged. "I don't know, but you can ask him yourself." He offered her a folded slip of paper. "Here's the hotel's phone number and address."

Savannah's scrutinous look passed from Anthony's alluring green eyes to the innocent-looking piece of paper in his outstretched hand.

"What do you mean you had to trace him to several different cities?" she asked. "And several different names?"

"Your boy's been all over the country in the last few months," Anthony said. He consulted a pad where he'd written notes. "I've found evidence of him being in St. Louis, Phoenix, Milwaukee, Charlotte, Memphis, Houston, and even Mexico City."

"Mexico City?" Savannah shook her head. "Dwayne used to always talk about wanting to visit Mexico City. Guess he made it," she said more to herself than to Anthony.

"As far as his aliases are concerned, Dwayne Dailey has become Kevin Edwards, Charles Nestor,

and currently"—he double-checked his notes—
"Randolph Mann."

"All those cities and all those names . . . it sounds
like he's running from something." Her thoughts
seemed to carry her far away from the waiting detective. After a few lost moments, she refocused on Anthony . . . more specifically on the slip of paper he
held out to her.

"I don't know if I want to talk to him," she whispered.

"What?" Anthony looked confused. "Why wouldn't
you want to talk to him?"

"And say what? 'So why'd you leave your family?' "
Savannah's tone was sarcastic.

"That would be a start," Anthony insisted. "Then
you could follow that with, 'So where's the money
you stole from me?' "

"I can't imagine that any answer he might have
would make a difference now." She doodled aim-
lessly on the desk blotter/calendar that covered the
desktop. "Anthony, all I've done these past few
months is try to rebuild my life and my family and
my business. It's been the hardest thing I've ever
done."

"And you've done a wonderful job. It's been in-
spiring to watch."

"Thank you." Savannah nodded slightly. "But my
point is I could only do that by looking and moving
forward. Going after Dwayne would be a huge step
backward. I'm not going to do it. He made his decision, and if he doesn't care any more about us than
that, then I say good riddance."

"Savannah, you hired me to find this guy—"

"No," Savannah quickly corrected him, "Sydney

hired you to find this guy. I never wanted Dwayne found. He made his feelings about his family and his business and his life abundantly clear when he left. What could he possibly say that would change any of that now?"

"You can't let him get away with this." Anthony was adamant. "He has to be held accountable for what he's done."

"Are you familiar with the concept of divine reciprocity?" Savannah looked up from her doodles to lock eyes with him. "Divine reciprocity simply says 'What goes around comes around.' I believe Dwayne will be held accountable for what he's done. There's no doubt in my mind about that. I just don't believe I'm the authority he's going to have to answer to."

"There is certainly some validity in what you're saying," Anthony conceded. "But are you willing to just let the universe take care of this for you? Don't you want to see him pay?"

Savannah pushed away from the desk and stood to face Anthony. "I have worked very hard these last few months to put my life and my family back together. I can't help but believe that seeing Dwayne at this point would only be disruptive. There's just nothing left to say."

Anthony shook his head in disbelief. "Are you at least going to divorce him?" Unconsciously he held his breath, anxious for her answer for reasons he couldn't—or wouldn't—identify.

Savannah paused to consider, her gaze fixed on some faraway sight. After a moment, she nodded. "I suppose that must be done. If for no other reason than to get all the legalities straightened out."

Anthony's breath released slowly. "Then you are

going to need this." He placed the folded paper on the corner of Savannah's desk. "If for no other reason than to serve him with divorce papers."

Savannah watched his movements but made no move to accept or reject the paper. She leaned back against the desk and folded her arms across her body. "So I guess that's it for you, right? Case closed?"

Anthony stood slightly to her side, his hands shoved in his pants pockets. "I guess it is," he said. His eyes met hers, searching for some sign that she wanted to see him again as much as he wanted to see her. He knew it was unreasonable, irrational. *I just tracked down a husband who abandoned her,* his rational mind pointed out. *The last thing she's going to be ready for is a man in her life.* He stood quietly, aware of her questioning look, but unable to make a move to leave or ask permission to stay. *This is crazy,* his heart screamed. *Do something!*

"Um, Savannah," he began tentatively, "I know this is lousy timing, but I would really like to see you again . . . personally . . . outside of this case . . . you know, take you to dinner or something." His voice trailed off as he finished the sentence. He looked away from her gaze, feeling very much like the awkward teenager he once was.

Savannah was silent, apparently taken aback by his words. "Um . . . I don't know what to say," she stammered. "How old are you?"

It was Anthony's turn to be taken aback. "How old am I? Wh . . . ? I'm old enough to buy you a drink. Why does it matter how old I am?"

She laughed slightly. "Well, it's just that I'm old enough to be your . . . older sister, and I can't imag-

ine why you would want to go out with me. You're
Jakarta's age, aren't you?"

"Well, I don't know what Jakarta's age is," Anthony said, "but I'm twenty-eight."

"Oh . . . I don't know how to respond to that. You
know, I'm thirty-eight . . . I'll be thirty-nine in two
months."

"Why does any of that matter?"

Savannah thought for a moment, and couldn't
come up with a single reason why it did. At least not
a single reason she cared about.

Anthony grew more nervous in her silence. "I'll
understand if you don't want to," he said. "I just
knew I'd never forgive myself if I didn't even ask. I
find you beautiful and fascinating and intelligent,
and I wanted to spend more time with you. But I'll
understand if that's not what you want."

Savannah looked him straight in the eye. "You
know what, Anthony, there was a time in my life, not
too very long ago, when I would have been very concerned about what other people thought." She unconsciously smoothed her hand over her natural do.
"But I've been through too much and I've worked
too hard to become who I am for that to matter
anymore. Why wouldn't I want to go out with you,
Anthony Martin? I am honored and flattered that
you asked. Thank you."

"I take it that was a yes." A slight smile appeared
on Anthony's face.

"Yes, yes, it was." Savannah returned his smile.
"Call me later to finalize the plans?"

"Absolutely." Anthony's smile had grown wider.
He put away his notepad, closed his briefcase, and
prepared to leave her office. "I'll talk to you soon."

After Anthony left, Savannah looked at the folded slip of paper he'd left on the edge of her desk. She tilted her head, trying to get a peek at the information inside without actually touching the paper. She could see a bit of his distinctive handwriting, but not enough to register in her mind as any kind of logical information. She leaned closer to it, still studiously not touching it, trying to get a better look.

"You're being silly," she admonished herself after a few moments of craning her neck. "Just pick up the damn paper. It won't bite." She sighed and grabbed for the paper. "Randolph Mann, Hotel Monteleone, Royal Street, New Orleans." Her lip curled as a slight sneer crossed her face. "New Orleans? Yet another entry on his list of 'places to go before I die.' Guess he's on the grand tour. With my money." Savannah shook her head in disgust and refolded the paper. She put the paper in the lap drawer of her desk.

Based on what Anthony has told me, Dwayne is probably not going to be in New Orleans for long. She sat down heavily in the leather office chair that Dwayne had specially ordered because of its ergonomic features, and looked around the office that Dwayne had specially designed to be impressive, until her gaze fell on the stack of paperwork that represented the tangle of overdue bills, irate employees, and half-finished contracts Dwayne had left in his wake. And then she accepted what she had to do.

"But not tonight," she decided. "I've waited this long to deal with Dwayne, I can wait a little longer. Tonight, I have other plans."

Eleven

"Come on, Savannah, you've got to be kidding me. Is this some kind of joke?" Sydney had stopped by Savannah's house to check on her and was horrified when she heard about Savannah's date. Savannah had chosen not to tell her sisters that Anthony had tracked down Dwayne, not quite ready to deal with the fireworks that would accompany that information.

"How could you even think about going out with that boy?" Sydney demanded.

"Boy?" Savannah gave her sister a disapproving look. "Anthony Martin is a highly respected professional. And he's twenty-eight years old."

"Uh-huh, same age as our baby sister," Sydney pointed out. "You know, Savannah, I can appreciate you wanting to go out and move on with your life, but shouldn't you be trying to find someone your own age? How is that going to look?"

"Sydney," Savannah said, "I could not possibly care less how it looks. But if I were to give it any thought, I would think it looks like 'that old woman must be *hot*, if she got that young boy to go out with her.' "

Sydney rolled her eyes. "Savannah, you can go out

and make a fool of yourself if you want to, but beyond the fact that that man is your employee—"

"Your employee," Savannah corrected quickly. "He is *your* employee . . . you paid him. Which reminds me, I should probably thank you for that. Because if you hadn't insisted on hiring a detective to track down Dwayne, I would never have met this remarkable young man. So thank you for that, Syd."

"Yeah, that's right, blame me." Sydney tried a different approach. "What do your children think about this? I mean really, Savannah, they're still dealing with the abandonment of their father, and here you go, dating this young man. I just don't think it's right."

Sydney's words gave Savannah pause. "You know, I actually did think about that. And then, I came to realize I'm just going out to dinner with the man. And I deserve a dinner with a handsome man who's interested in me. These last few months have been hell on me, and if anybody knows that, it would be D.J. and Stephanie. So what I hope my children will think is 'Way to go, Mom.' "

Jakarta entered the room and caught the last of Sydney's words. "Way to go, Mom, what?" she said. "What cha up to?"

"Yes, Savannah," Sydney drawled. "Tell your baby sister what you're up to."

Savannah flashed Sydney a look. "It's no big deal, J. Anthony asked me to go out with him and I'm going."

"Isn't that horrible?" Sydney demanded of Jakarta. "I mean really, she's ten years older than he is. And she's still a married woman for all intents and purposes."

Savannah and Jakarta favored Sydney with matching glares.

"Well, okay," Sydney backed down slightly. "That married thing is probably not the best reason. Still, he's so much younger than you. And he's an employee, for God's sake. He's the help! You're going out with the help!"

"Aw, get over it, Syd," Jakarta said. "I think it's great. He's a fine man, and I hope you have a fabulous time." Jakarta looked slyly at Savannah. "Been a long time, hasn't it, sis? Nothing quite like a fine man to help a woman climb back up on the horse."

"Jakarta!" Savannah and Sydney both said.

"It is not that kind of party, J," Savannah assured her. "He's a handsome man who's asked me out to dinner and I'm going."

"Well, if it turns out to be that kind of party," Jakarta said, smiling, "you have a good time."

"I should have known you would react this way," Sydney said. "You are, after all, the wild child, aren't you, J?"

"Hey, I just know how to live life, Syd. Whenever you're ready for that lesson, you let me know."

Sydney rolled her eyes. "Well, what about Paris? Let's call Paris and see what she thinks. Paris will make you see how silly this is."

Savannah shook her head. "Sydney, this is not a committee decision. I'm going out on a date with a handsome man. And I suggest you make your peace with it."

Sydney threw her hands up. "I don't know what to do with either of you. I want to be on the record saying I think this is a bad idea."

Savannah shrugged. "Duly noted. Now, if you'll

excuse me, my date will be here soon." She smiled and strolled into the bathroom to shower.

After the conversation with her sisters, Savannah was dreading talking to her children, but she knew it had to be done. After her shower, she found her children sprawled out in the family room watching TV.

"Guys, can we talk for a second?" she said.

"Sure, Mom, what's up?" D.J. answered.

"Hit the mute button for a second please. I need to talk to you guys about something."

D.J. muted the TV as his mother asked, and the kids turned expectant faces toward their mother.

"What's up, Mom?" Stephanie asked.

"I just wanted to let you two know that I'm going out on a date tonight."

"A date?" D.J. said.

"With who?" Stephanie demanded.

"You know him," Savannah replied calmly. "Anthony Martin, that detective your Aunt Sydney hired to help us find—that detective who's been working with us." Savannah studiously avoided mentioning their father.

"He's kinda young for you, isn't he, Mom?" Stephanie said.

"He's not that much younger than I am," Savannah replied defensively. "But I just wanted you guys to know that I'm going out. We can talk about how you're feeling about it if you'd like."

D.J. hit the mute button again, turning the volume back up on the TV. "What difference does it make how we feel about it, Mom? It's your life . . . if you want to go out, go out."

"I wanted you to be okay with this," she said. "I

want you to feel comfortable. There have been a lot of changes in our lives these last few months, and I don't want to do anything that's going to cause you more pain."

Stephanie smiled at her mother. "Mom, you going out will not cause us pain. Go on out and have a good time. You've earned it."

D.J. didn't answer.

"So, D.J., what are your thoughts?" Savannah asked him directly.

"I've told you, Mom, if you want to go out, go out." His focus was on the channels he was surfing through, not Savannah.

"It seems like you're not okay with this," Savannah tried again.

"Mom, really, it doesn't matter. You go on out and do whatever you want to do."

Savannah said, "All right. But if you decide you want to talk about it, let me know."

"Talk about what?" D.J. said. "What's the point of talking about it. You're going to do what you want anyway!"

"D.J.!" Savannah was shocked at his outburst. "What is wrong with you?"

"Nothing, Mom. Just forget it." D.J. looked away sullenly.

"No, D.J., I don't think I can. What's wrong?"

"Okay, you asked." He hit the mute button again and turned to face her. "I don't see how you can even be thinking about going out. Daddy's missing. We don't know what's going on with him. And you're his wife. And here you are, going out on a date. It's just not right."

Savannah sighed and walked toward her son.

"Baby," she said softly, "your daddy is not missing . . . your daddy ran away. That's completely different. Missing implies that he went against his will or that there was some foul play involved. That's not what happened here and you know that. Your daddy left, and left us to pick up the pieces. Now I understand if this is a hard thing for you to accept, but please, please don't act like I'm somehow betraying your father by moving on with my life, because I am not trying to hear that."

D.J. looked defiant. "I still don't think it's right. I'm sorry, Mom, I just don't. You are still married, aren't you? And sooner or later Daddy will be coming home and he's going to want us to be a family again."

Savannah shook her head sadly. "D.J., I don't think your dad is coming home, and I've got to be honest with you, even if he did we'll never be a family again. Too much has happened, too much time has passed." She squared her shoulders. "Now, I am going out with Anthony. It's just dinner . . . it doesn't mean anything more than that. And I wanted you guys to know."

She leaned in to kiss her son's cheek, but he flinched away. "Okay," she said sadly, "I understand." And then she left the room. As she was walking down the hallway, she heard Stephanie admonish her older brother.

"D.J., how could you?" Stephanie sounded dismayed.

Savannah continued her walk down the hallway, not wanting to eavesdrop on the children. Savannah fervently hoped that whatever Stephanie said to her brother would help D.J. come to terms with this new page in their lives.

I'll help him however I can, she decided, *but I have to live my life, too. I can't put my life on hold for another Dwayne Dailey . . . even if it's my son.*

When she reached her bedroom, she found Jakarta going through her closet. "What's up, J?" Savannah asked.

"Oh, just looking for the perfect dress for your big date." Jakarta held two dresses aloft. "I've narrowed it down to these."

"Where's Sydney?"

"Oh, she left, grumbling under her breath all the way out the door, while you were talking to the kids." Jakarta shook her head dismissively. "Forget about Sydney. She's got issues that have nothing to do with you. We need to pick a dress—right now. Anthony will be here soon."

"Why are you so gung-ho for this?" Savannah asked her youngest sister. "It's almost as if you have something vested in me going out with Anthony."

Jakarta paused for a moment, pondering the question. "I guess I'm just really happy to see you start living your life—finally," she said. "My whole life you've always seemed to be a grown-up to me, even though you are only ten years older. My earliest memories are of you taking care of all of us. And then you married and took care of your husband and children. You never seemed to be a kid—free and loose and enjoying yourself. That's what I want for you now. I'm so happy to see you letting your hair down—or chopping your hair off as the case may be"—Jakarta laughed—"and enjoying life. Maybe I won't be the only wild Raven sister from now on."

"I don't think 'wild' is in my future." Savannah giggled. "But I guess you're right, I have always been mothering and caring for and looking out for everybody else. I'm not sure I know how to do it any other way."

Jakarta handed her sister a fire-engine-red dress. "Well, now's an excellent time to find out."

Savannah nodded and slipped into the dress. Jakarta tied the sash at Savannah's hip and stepped back to admire the results.

"You look beautiful, sis."

"Thank you, Jakarta, I take that as high praise coming from you."

Savannah looked in the mirror and had to admit she did look very good. The dress Jakarta had picked was elegant and sexy at the same time. It was a wrap dress made of slinky, clingy fabric, crossing between her breasts and tying at the waist. Jakarta insisted Savannah wear silver hoop earrings and a simple silver chain necklace. Savannah's hair had been freshly trimmed by Jakarta into a stylish natural Afro.

"I really like my hair like this," Savannah muttered. "I wonder why it took me so long." She turned in the mirror to get a view of the back.

"Yeah, you look good coming and going." Jakarta giggled. "Anthony won't know what hit him."

"I don't know, J, he's so handsome . . . he's probably got women falling all over him. I still can't figure out why he'd want to go out with me."

"I don't know if that's for you to figure out," Jakarta said. "Don't question it, sis, just roll with it . . . enjoy it. You're only going to dinner with this guy. Stop trying to find the meaning of life in one dinner."

"Okay, okay. You're right." Savannah turned from the mirror and grabbed a small evening bag off the bed. "Wish me luck."

"Hey, wait a minute! Where are you going?" Jakarta looked horrified.

"I'm going to wait for my date. He'll be here any minute."

"You're not going to answer the door, are you?"

Savannah didn't bother to try and hide the confusion on her face. "Well, of course I'm going to answer the door."

"Oh, no." Jakarta rushed to block the bedroom door. "You have to wait here so you can make a grand entrance when he arrives."

"That's just silly, Jakarta," Savannah protested. "I'm ready to go. Why should I act like I'm not?"

"Look, Savannah, it's been a long time since you've been on a date, so you're going to have to trust me on this. An entrance is the way to go."

"Jakarta, that's juvenile, and I'm not going to do it. Now step aside."

Reluctantly, Jakarta allowed Savannah to leave the bedroom. "You're making a mistake," she called out to her sister's retreating back.

"I'm sure it's the first of many," Savannah mumbled.

Twelve

Anthony was unexpectedly nervous as he prepared for his date with Savannah. As handsome as he was, dating was not something he usually did. Anthony found often that his business took too much of his time and he had come to discover that he had little patience for the dating game as it seemed to exist in the world. So even though he was, what would be considered by any standards, a "good catch," he did not often go out. But this date was very different. This date he anticipated very much. He really wanted to impress Savannah, and he wasn't really even sure why. The age difference didn't bother him, but he thought it might trouble her. So he dressed with particular care, wanting to appear as mature and responsible as possible.

Anthony left his apartment to pick up Savannah with plenty of time to spare, not wanting to be late for this very special evening. As he navigated his car through town, he passed a flower vendor on the street.

"Flowers?" he wondered. "Is that cute or tacky?" Deciding it might make him look too anxious, Anthony passed on the flowers. Shortly he arrived at Savannah's house and parked his car on the brick driveway. He hesitated to get out of the car, nerves wracking his confidence. *This is ridiculous,* he admonished himself. *I'm acting like a kid. It's just a date. So why is this one so much different?* he demanded of his psyche. *Why am I sweating this one so much?* No answers came. As he nervously cupped his hands and blew into them checking his breath, he decided to walk the walk. *If I can't actually be calm, at least I can look* calm. He steeled his nerves, climbed out of the car, and walked up to her stoop.

He rang the bell, fully expecting to encounter one of Savannah's entourage—sisters and/or children—but was pleasantly surprised when Savannah opened the door herself.

"Good evening." She smiled. "You're right on time."

"And so are you." Anthony returned her smile. "I guess I expected to have to wait."

Savannah gave a small, self-conscious laugh. "Nope, no grand entrances tonight. Although that was Jakarta's recommendation. But for me, I decided I'm just too old for games like that."

"Just too old?" Anthony shook his head. "You make it sound like you have one foot in the nursing home."

"You know," Savannah said, cocking her head to the side, "there's no point in us trying to ignore it. I am much older than you."

Anthony sighed. "Not this again."

"Well, it's true, Anthony. Not talking about it doesn't make it not true."

"Define 'much older,' " he insisted.

"We're ten years apart. Ten years is a decade," she countered. "Hell, it's almost a generation."

Anthony shook his head. "You're exaggerating,

Savannah. And do we have to have this conversation on the porch? If we have to keep talking about this, could we please continue it over dinner?"

With a start, Savannah suddenly realized they were still standing outside. "I'm sorry. I'm completely out of practice with this kind of thing," she said. "I'm ready to go if you are."

"I am most definitely ready to go." Anthony motioned toward his car. Savannah closed the door to her house and crossed the driveway. Anthony hurried ahead of her and opened the car door. She smiled at the courtly gesture as she slid into the low seat. She had to admit to being surprised by his choice of car.

"I would have figured you for a flashy car like a Corvette or a Porsche," she observed when he climbed in next to her.

Anthony laughed. "Not really effective in my line of work," he said. "I need to be able to sneak up on people and spy on them unnoticed. People tend to notice and remember a bright red Porsche."

"Guess I hadn't thought of it that way," Savannah conceded. "So you chose a gray Chevy because it's nondescript?"

"Pretty much." Anthony started the car. "I hope you like Thai food."

"I'm not sure if I do or not," Savannah said honestly. "But I'm sure I'm willing to give it a try."

"Can't ask for more than that." Anthony nodded.

Shortly, they arrived at the restaurant. Savannah was impressed by the colorful Asian décor. Anthony gave the hostess his name and she confirmed his reservation. The pair was led to a low table with plump, colorful cushions surrounding it.

"We sit on the floor?" Savannah tried to conceal her incredulity.

"I hope that's okay?" Anthony looked concerned.

Savannah shrugged. "Sure . . . why not?"

Once they were settled at the table, the hostess handed out the menus.

"What do you recommend?" Savannah asked.

"We should start with the spring rolls," Anthony suggested. "And then *satay*, which is sort of like chicken shish kebab, then *kaeng khiao wan nuea*, the green curry with beef, and *mi krop*, the crispy noodles."

"Wow, you said that like a native," Savannah marveled. "Guess you've eaten here before."

Anthony nodded. "Once or twice. So does that food sound okay?"

"It sounds fine." Savannah closed her menu and set it on the table. "Why don't you place that order for us?"

Anthony nodded, pleased with her confidence. After he'd given the waitress their order, Anthony focused his attention on Savannah.

"So, tell me about yourself," he said.

Savannah frowned slightly. "I don't know what I could tell you that you don't already know. I mean, my life is pretty much an open book these days . . . especially to you."

"Your life is more than this episode with your husband," Anthony insisted. "What about the rest of it?"

Savannah sat quietly for a few moments, the corner of her bottom lip clenched between her teeth as she pondered his question.

"I'm not sure that my life is more than this episode," she said finally. "Before Dwayne disappeared, my whole life was him and my family. After he disappeared, my whole life became cleaning up after him and trying to hold my family and business together." She gave a huge sigh. "And now that you've found him, my whole life is about to be exacting justice and repayment for what he's done. So it seems I am very much defined by this episode." Her shoulders slumped as the weight of her words settled on her. "Damn," she whispered softly.

"What is it?" he asked.

Savannah sighed. "I'm probably going to have to do something about him now, aren't I?"

"I'm not sure what you mean." Anthony tried to deflect the question.

"Well, you've found him—we know where he is. I can't just ignore that. It's not like he's going to go away," she said resentfully. "I mean, he would love to go away, but there are legalities that have to be dealt with, aren't there?" She rolled her eyes in disgust. "I swear, I can't even get away from the man for one evening," she muttered.

A feeling of helplessness rushed over Anthony. *What have I done?* his mind screamed.

"Savannah, I'm sorry," he said. "The last thing I wanted to do was bring you down. I had hoped that taking you to dinner would help you forget about the situation, at least for a while."

Savannah nodded. "Yeah, me too. But I guess the situation is never too far away from my thoughts."

At that moment, their dinner arrived. They stopped talking as the waitress laid the dishes in front of them.

Once the waitress left the table, Anthony tried to

lighten the mood. "You up for using chopsticks?" he asked.

Savannah managed a weak smile, but for all intents and purposes it was too late. Her carefree mood was shattered.

"I'd probably better use a fork," she said. "I don't want to end up wearing this dinner instead of eating it."

Anthony nodded and set the chopsticks on the table. They began their meal, eating in strained silence, only casual comments about the food passing between them.

When dinner was over, Anthony quickly paid the check and they left the restaurant. He would have liked to linger over dessert, but it was obvious that for Savannah, the night was over.

They were very quiet during the ride home. After he pulled into her driveway, he realized he couldn't take it anymore.

"I'm sorry that you didn't enjoy yourself this evening, Savannah," he apologized. "I wanted tonight to be special."

"It's not your fault," Savannah tried to reassure him. "In fact, it actually doesn't have much to do with you. There's some unfinished business I need to handle," she said. "And until I handle it, it's not going to go away."

Anthony nodded. "I do understand that," he said. "I'd just hoped that tonight would give you a brief vacation from your unfinished business."

"Some things you just can't hide from," she said. "Good night, Anthony."

"Good night, Savannah," he replied.

As he watched her reach for the door handle, he

wanted to try and confirm another date or simply ask if he could call her again, but his every instinct told him now was not the time. He also struggled with his desire to kiss her, but there was no question that that would be an inappropriate action.

He was pleasantly surprised when she reached across the seat of the car and gently squeezed his hand.

"It was a lovely evening," she said.

"Well, that's not really true, but thank you for saying so," Anthony replied.

Savannah smiled slightly and let herself out of the car. With sadness, Anthony watched her unlock the front door and disappear into her house.

"Well, so much for that date," he muttered wryly, realizing all over again why it was that he didn't date very often. With a fleeting sense of disappointment over what might have been, Anthony started his car and backed out of her driveway.

Savannah stood in her foyer and listened as Anthony left. "Damn," she swore softly. "I completely ruined that evening. Anthony Martin will never want to see me again."

Why is Dwayne still such a presence in my life? I should be through with this . . . how long has it been? He left me. Why can't I let him go?

Annoyed, she realized that her relationship with Dwayne was far from being over. "Closure," she whispered, "I need closure to end this completely. And I know exactly how to get it."

She went into the study and got her briefcase. Opening the soft leather attaché, she dug around among the pens, pencils, folders, and other business paraphernalia until she found what she was looking for. She pulled out the slip of paper with Anthony's handwriting on it.

"Randolph Mann, Hotel Monteleon, Royal Street, New Orleans," she read aloud.

I wonder what New Orleans is like this time of year?

Savannah began making preparations immediately.

When Jakarta walked past Savannah's bedroom on her way to the kitchen for a late night snack, she was stopped short by the sight of an open suitcase on her sister's bed.

"What's going on, Savannah?" Jakarta poked her head in the bedroom.

"Jakarta, good. I was just about to come find you. I have to go out of town for a few days."

"You're going away? Now?" Jakarta was stunned.

"I'll only be gone a day or so. You can handle the kids for that long, right?" Savannah did not look up from the toiletry bag she was packing.

"Of course I can," Jakarta said. "That's not the issue. Are you sure this is the right time for you to be going away?"

Savannah crossed the bedroom to drop the toiletry bag into her suitcase. "Yes," she said tersely. "This has to be done."

"What, Savannah? What has to be done?" Jakarta watched her sister's decisive movements with growing concern. "Where are you going?"

"Relax, J. I know what I'm doing. See you in a couple of days." Savannah zipped her suitcase and headed toward the door, leaving a confused sister in her wake.

Thirteen

What a beautiful city, she thought. As she rode in a cab from the airport, she couldn't help reflecting on the character and quality of New Orleans. *If this were some other time. And maybe even some other person.* She smiled as thoughts of Anthony passed through her mind. The smile slowly faded from her face as she turned her thoughts to the mission ahead. She looked down again at the folded slip of paper and noted again the name of the hotel.

Wonder if it's a nice place, she thought. *Certainly sounds elegant. And Lord knows he's got enough money to fund "elegant."* She shook her head, scattering the thoughts, wanting her mind to be clear for this meeting. She took a deep breath and leaned back against the seat of the cab.

"First time in New Orleans?" The cab driver attempted conversation.

"Yes," Savannah answered tersely. "Never had a need to be here before now."

"A need?" the cab driver questioned. "Is everything okay, miss?"

Savannah sat silently, pondering the question, formulating an answer.

"Everything is about to be just fine," she said finally. She looked away, sending what she hoped was a clear signal to the cab driver that the conversation was over. Thankfully, the cabbie took the hint, shrugged his shoulders, and turned his attention back to the road. Savannah watched as the city sped by, not really noticing the scenery this time, instead visualizing the confrontation ahead. Before she was fully ready, the cab arrived.

"Hotel Monteleon," the driver announced. Savannah, grim-faced and determined, handed the driver the fare and climbed out of the cab without comment. The hotel was in the famous French Quarter. Savannah was struck by the old-world beauty and grace of the hotel. She walked into the lobby and was greeted by an enormous center table with a beautiful and obviously expensive fresh flower arrangement. Her heels sounded on the marble floor as she strode purposefully to the front desk.

"I am looking for one of your guests," she told the young woman at the counter. "I need the room of Dwa—um, Randolph Mann." The fake name tasted disgusting in her mouth.

The woman hesitated. "I can't give you a room number," she said. "But if you go to the house phone"—she pointed out an ornate phone on a table across the lobby—"you can call the hotel operator and she'll connect you to the guest's room."

Savannah nodded. "Whatever." She crossed to the house phone, dialed, and said in clipped tones, "Randolph Mann's room please."

After a brief pause and a series of clicks, the phone began to ring. With each ring, she practiced what she would say when he answered. After eight rings—she had meticulously counted each one—the hotel operator came back on.

"The party is not answering; would you like to leave a message?"

"No," Savannah said, "no message. I'll try again later." A frightening thought hit Savannah. "Mr. Mann is still a guest at the hotel, isn't he?"

"Yes, ma'am. Mr. Mann is still one of our registered guests," the operator replied.

"Thank you," Savannah said as a rush of relief coursed through her. She hung up the phone and pondered her next move. She decided to wait in the lobby. *I'll see him when he comes past,* she thought. *He will talk to me today.* She picked a secluded corner of the lobby that had a full view of the front doors and settled in to wait. *How long am I willing to wait?* Savannah wondered as she sat in the elegant hotel lobby turning over in her mind what she would say to her wayward husband. *It's been eight months. What will I say to him, what will he say to me?* She began to feel some of the anger that everyone in her life thought she should feel. As she thought about the events of the last eight months, the enormity of Dwayne's actions struck her with the force of a blow to the stomach.

I've been so busy trying to put my life back together, I haven't really allowed myself any time to think about what happened, she realized. *That son of a bitch just left and left me with the children and the business and the bills— and apparently never intended to see me again. How do you do that to somebody? How do you do that to somebody you've been married to and supposedly loved for seventeen years? How does that happen?*

As she sat and waited for him, the question of "What will I say to him?" became abundantly clear. She drew herself up to her fullest height and sat regally in the hotel chair. *Oh, yeah,* she thought. *I've*

got a few things to say to "Mr. Randolph Mann." At that
moment, Savannah decided she would wait as long
as she needed to, as long as it took.

*The sun is not going to set on this day without my
having told Dwayne exactly what I think about him.*

As her third hour of waiting in the lobby neared,
a commotion near the entrance drew her attention.

"Giselle, my belle! Any messages?"

The clerk at the front desk gave a girlish giggle.
"Oh, Mr. Mann, you so silly!" She leaned on the
counter in an obviously flirtatious position.

Savannah's eyes narrowed and her blood ran cold
at the sight of him. *So cool, so relaxed, so confident. And
good Lord, he looks good. . . .* The thought flashed in
her mind before she had a chance to rein it in. *I
guess eight months of carefree livin' large has agreed with
him,* she thought caustically.

Dwayne Dailey was a tall man, easily topping six-
two. His skin was smooth and a rich dark chocolate
color. He had gained a few pounds, Savannah noted.
Not enough to make him be considered fat, just
enough to indicate that he'd been living a pretty
leisurely life these last few months. Savannah noticed
he had grown a beard, something he professed to
hate all during their marriage. *No doubt all a part of
his disguise,* she figured. He had grown his hair long
and had it chemically straightened and pulled back
into a short ponytail at the nape of his neck. She
caught sight of a pinky ring on his hand as he waved
to someone across the room. She couldn't be sure,
but the sparkle of the ring indicated it was probably
expensive.

She watched from her secluded position as Dwayne
made his way across the lobby greeting every member

of the hotel staff as if they were old friends. As he pushed the elevator call button, Savannah stood and stepped out from the shadows.

"Hello, Dwayne." Calmly controlled fury emanated from her every pore. "Long time no see."

She was immediately rewarded by the shocked expression on his face.

"Savannah," he breathed. "What are you doing here?"

Savannah snorted. "I think the better question might be, what are *you* doing here?"

"I can explain."

"I doubt that very seriously," Savannah said, "but just out of pure curiosity, I'm going to give you a chance to try." Savannah glared at him. "How could you have done that to us? How could you? What kind of man does that to his family?"

"Savannah, you don't understand."

"Damn right I don't understand," Savannah snapped. Her brows drew together in rage. "I can't even pretend to understand. How can there be any understanding?"

"Savannah, at least let me try to explain—"

"You know, Dwayne, after all this time you've had to think about this, I would expect you to have a better explanation by now. But I guess you never expected to have to explain it . . . you never expected to see me again, did you? You figured you'd just change your name and become Randolph Mann and gallivant all over the world and we'd never find you—right?"

"I didn't think it all the way through, Savannah, obviously."

"Seems like you thought it through enough to

leave me with all the bills, to leave me with the family and the business and the employees to deal with."

The rage that Savannah had struggled to hold at bay all the months of her recovery, all the months that she had worked to put her life back together, was unleashed with a vengeance.

"I loved you, I gave my life to you, and you left in the night like a coward. How do you do something like that?" Savannah was unaware of the fact that her voice had gotten louder and louder. Dwayne looked around uncomfortably, realizing they were attracting attention in the lobby.

"Savannah, please calm down."

"Calm down? How do you even have the nerve to wrap your lips around 'calm down'? Out of all the things I would expect you to say to me, 'calm down' would be the last one!" She was a full roar now, not even completely aware that her rage had bubbled over.

Dwayne tried to move her toward the elevator as he insistently pushed on the call button. "Just come to my room so we can talk about this, please?"

"No, I don't think so!" she shouted.

"Savannah, please, I can explain." He looked around, embarrassed at the attention they were attracting.

Savannah gave him a withering look, the true personification of the expression "if looks could kill."

"I just can't think of anything I want to hear from you," she said.

"Please, Savannah. You've come all this way, at least give me a chance to explain." Dwayne's tone was just the right mixture of contrition and begging.

By then, the elevator Dwayne had called for arrived. "Just come upstairs with me. *Please.*"

Savannah's expression softened slightly as she reacted to the pleading in his voice. He reached for her arm. His touch immediately made her rage resurface. Savannah jerked her arm savagely from his grasp.

"Don't touch me! Don't you ever touch me again!"

He held his hands up in front of his chest and nodded in the direction of the elevator. As she stalked past him into the waiting elevator, Savannah glared at him. Dwayne followed her. As the door closed, the calm, contrite facade Dwayne had on display melted away.

"Bitch!" he growled. "You have no business here. You're right . . . I didn't ever think I'd see you again. Why are you here? Didn't you get the message when I left?"

"Why, you two-faced, crazy, good-for-nothing . . ." Savannah snarled through her teeth. "Don't you ever talk to me like that again. I came here to get an explanation. I came here to hear what you might have to say, for the sake of the children if nothing else. But you know what? It doesn't matter anymore."

She pushed the elevator's emergency stop button. "I got what I came here for. I know now everything I need to know. Good-bye, Dwayne." The door opened and she stepped off the elevator. "You don't ever have to worry about me bothering you again. The next thing you'll hear from me will be divorce papers."

She watched with a deep sense of satisfaction as

the elevator doors closed, blocking out his face. *Man, that felt good,* she thought. Rather than wait for the elevator to return, she took the fire-exit stairs, walked down the few flights, and exited at the side of the building.

Done, she decided. *It's time to go home.* She held out her arm to hail a cab to take her back to the airport. *Time to get on with my new life . . . this part is finished.*

When the cab arrived, she settled into it, smiling. "Airport please," she said, "I'm going home."

Fourteen

All the way to her house from the airport, Savannah's thoughts focused on her children. *Do I tell them that I've seen their father?* she wondered. *How much do they deserve to know? Would it comfort them to know that he's still alive? Or would it anger them to realize that he's still alive and he has completely abandoned us? Is it fair to still let them hold out hope?*

They were questions with no answers. When she arrived at home, D.J. and Stephanie were still at school. Putting aside her concerns about them for the moment, Savannah made her first call to the business.

"Hi, Paul, this is Savannah. How are things?"

"Oh, hey, Mrs. Dailey," Paul said cheerfully. "Everything's going great. Got some guys out at the Williams job, and there's another crew out working in the Atlas Building downtown."

"That's music to my ears," Savannah said. "Thanks for holding down the fort while I was gone. And, Paul . . . I've told you before—call me Savannah."

"Sorry . . . old habits die hard. So how was your trip?" Paul asked.

"Very productive," Savannah said. "Very productive, indeed. Listen, since it sounds like everything's under control down there, I'm going to take the rest of the day off. See you in the morning?"

"Sure, Mrs. Dailey—um, I mean Savannah. No problem."

Savannah hung up the phone and allowed herself a brief moment of reflection on how far she had come. Then she made another call.

"Martin Investigations, Anthony Martin speaking."

She smiled at the sound of his voice.

"Hello, Anthony Martin," she said with mock formality, "this is Savannah Raven."

"Savannah! What a pleasant surprise."

"Is it a surprise really?" Savannah asked.

"Well, yeah," Anthony answered. "I wasn't sure if I'd hear from you again. I thought that last week we might have had our first and last date."

The line hummed quietly in the ensuing silence.

"So," Anthony said, clearing his throat, "what can I do for you?"

Savannah took a deep breath and decided to go for it. "Actually, Anthony, I was calling to see if we might try that date thing again."

"Oh?" Anthony's tone was hopeful.

"Well, I wasn't at my best when we went out the first time . . . I was way too distracted by other things," Savannah admitted. "But I have taken care of some business that was weighing on my head, and if you're still willing to take a chance, I'd love to have dinner with you again."

"That would be fabulous," Anthony said. "What are you doing tonight?"

Savannah laughed. "So quickly?"

"Well, what's the point in waiting?" he asked. "Unless of course you have plans."

"No, no plans," Savannah said quickly. "Tonight would be great."

Anthony said, "I'll be there at seven to pick you up."

"Where are we going?"

"I don't know yet," Anthony answered, "but it will be someplace really special. I sense you're a woman who needs a celebration."

Savannah smiled at his thoughtfulness. "You have no idea. I'll see you tonight." She hung up the phone, the smile still beaming on her face.

What are you doing? her conscience demanded. *You've barely gotten out of your marriage and now you're going after this young man?*

"He's a handsome, successful man who wants to go out with me." Her voice broke the quiet, scattering the annoying thoughts. "He's free, single, and over twenty-one," she said, laughing. "I'm going for it."

She went to her bedroom to pick out an outfit for the night ahead.

Anthony was determined that this date go better than their previous one. His professional job for Savannah was over, and he made up his mind that he was not going to mention Dwayne, or New Orleans, or Dailey Plumbing, or anything else that might upset Savannah.

"It's a brand-new day," he said to his reflection in the bathroom mirror. "And I'm going to make the most of it." As he shaved the day's stubble away, he replayed their previous date in his mind.

"I think I tried too hard," he decided. "So this time, I'm just going to relax." He headed into his bedroom, reached into his drawer, and selected a rich purple polo-style shirt. He pulled the casual shirt on over his head and put on the attitude that would be his for the evening.

"Whatever will be will be."

When Anthony arrived at Savannah's house, again she was ready and waiting for him.

"Hi," she said as she opened the door. "I'm so glad we're going to do this again."

"Me, too," he agreed. "I really feel like tonight is going to be different."

Savannah nodded. "So do I. And do you know why?"

"Well, I know why I feel that way, but I would be interested in knowing why you feel that way."

"I'll make a deal with you," she said. "How 'bout I tell you in the car on the way to this great Italian restaurant I know?" She paused. "Unless you had somewhere else in mind."

"No." Anthony was quick to agree with her plan. "I didn't have anything at all in mind; in fact, I was planning to ask you what you wanted."

"I want Italian tonight," she said flirtatiously, fully aware of his ethnicity.

They got into the car, and she gave him directions to the restaurant. Once they started on their way, he turned to her and said, "Okay now. Tell me why you're convinced that this night is going to be different."

"Well," she began slowly, "because I'm very different on this night."

Anthony nodded. "I could sense a change from the moment you called me this afternoon."

"That's very perceptive of you, Detective Martin," she teased. "I see why you have such a great reputation as an investigator."

He laughed with her. "Well, maybe my detective skills aren't all that, because I'm not sure why there's a change in you."

Savannah smiled. "That part's easy. I took your advice and I went to New Orleans."

"You did what?" Anthony slammed on the brakes, bringing the car to an abrupt halt. "When did you go to New Orleans?"

"I just got back earlier today," she said. "After our first date went so poorly, I had to ask myself what the problem was. I came to realize that even though I wanted to believe I was completely finished with Dwayne Dailey, the truth of the matter was, I wasn't. I tried to convince myself I was, but the simple reality was until I had had it out with Dwayne, I would never truly be free of him. So I found him in New Orleans—right where you said he'd be, by the way—and confronted him." Savannah took a deep breath. "Long story short, I now have no doubts that Dwayne Dailey is out of my life. And I wanted to celebrate . . . with you."

Anthony looked at her, surprise etched on his features. "I don't know what to say," he managed.

"Don't say anything," Savannah urged. "Just start the car rolling again, so we can get to the restaurant. I'm famished."

As if suddenly realizing the car was stopped in the

middle of the street, Anthony quickly jerked the gearshift into drive and started back down the road.

Savannah smiled, secretly pleased that she had been able to surprise him so. Once they were seated at the restaurant, Savannah began flirting mercilessly with him. Amused by her behavior and remembering his "whatever will be will be" mantra, Anthony played along.

Savannah felt alive—more alive than she remembered feeling, maybe ever. She watched his hands as he handled his utensils. The task that should have been mundane seemed electrifying somehow to Savannah because her senses were so heightened. She lowered her head and peered through her lashes, watching as he lifted food to his mouth, watching the movements of his jaw and lips as he chewed. She wanted to look away, felt a little silly studying him so, but she couldn't. She was thoroughly entranced. After a few moments, her intense scrutiny seemed to make Anthony uncomfortable.

"What?" he asked. "Have I got some food in my teeth?"

Savannah chuckled self-consciously. "No, everything's fine."

"So why are you staring at me?"

"Well, so much for my powers of surveillance," she said. "I called myself sneaking a look at you."

"Why don't you leave the surveillance to the pros?" He laughed. "But really, why are you looking at me so closely?"

A half dozen responses passed through Savannah's mind. She considered deflecting the question with a joke, or hiding her true intentions with an outright lie. But somehow she couldn't generate

An important message from the ARABESQUE Editor

Dear Arabesque Reader,

Because you've chosen to read one of our Arabesque romance novels, we'd like to say "thank you"! And, as a special way to thank you, we've selected four more of the books you love so well to send you for FREE!

Please enjoy them with our compliments, and thank you for continuing to enjoy Arabesque...the soul of romance.

Karen Thomas
Senior Editor,
Arabesque Romance Novels

Check out our website at
www.arabesquebooks.com

SPECIAL OFFER!
4 FREE BOOKS

ARABESQUE ®
A PRODUCT OF
★BET BOOKS™

3 QUICK STEPS
TO RECEIVE YOUR "THANK YOU" GIFT
FROM THE EDITOR

Send this card back and you'll receive 4 FREE Arabesque
novels! The introductory shipment of 4 Arabesque novels – a
$23.96 value – is yours absolutely FREE!

There's no catch. You're under no obligation to buy anything.
You'll receive your introductory shipment of 4 Arabesque
novels absolutely FREE (plus $1.50 to offset the costs of
shipping & handling). And you don't have to make any
minimum number of purchases—not even one!

We hope that after receiving your books you'll want to
remain an Arabesque subscriber. But the choice is yours to
continue or cancel, anytime at all! So why not take us up on
our invitation to receive 4 Arabesque Romance Novels, with
no risk of any kind. You'll be glad you did!

Call us
TOLL-FREE
at 1-800-770-1963

THE EDITOR'S "THANK YOU" GIFT INCLUDES:

- 4 books absolutely FREE (plus $1.50 for shipping and handling)
- A FREE newsletter, *Arabesque Romance News*, filled with author interviews, book previews, special offers, and more!
- No risks or obligations. You're free to cancel whenever you wish... with no questions asked.

BOOK CERTIFICATE

Yes! Please send me 4 FREE Arabesque novels (plus $1.50 for shipping & handling). I understand I am under no obligation to purchase any books, as explained on the back of this card.

Name _____

Address _____ Apt. _____

City _____ State _____ Zip _____

Telephone ( ) _____

Signature _____

Offer limited to one per household and not valid to current subscribers. All orders subject to approval. Terms, offer, & price subject to change. Offer valid only in the U.S.

AN042A

Thank you!

Accepting the four introductory books for FREE (plus $1.50 to offset the cost of shipping & handling) places you under no obligation to buy anything. You may keep the books and return the shipping statement marked "cancelled". If you do not cancel, about a month later we will send 4 additional Arabesque novels, and you will be billed the preferred subscriber's price of just $4.00 per title. That's $16.00 for all 4 books for a savings of 33% off the cover price (Plus $1.50 for shipping and handling). You may cancel at any time, but if you choose to continue, every month we'll send you 4 more books, which you may either purchase at the preferred discount price. . . or return to us and cancel your subscription.

THE ARABESQUE ROMANCE CLUB: HERE'S HOW IT WORKS

ARABESQUE ROMANCE BOOK CLUB
P.O. Box 5214
Clifton NJ 07015-5214

PLACE
STAMP
HERE

those words. Somehow, she knew nothing but the truth would do.

"I think you are the sexiest man I have ever been this close to," she said honestly. "I find myself fascinated by the movements of your hands and mouth."

Anthony looked shocked, pleased, and flattered all at the same time. "Oh," he managed.

I've come this far, Savannah thought. *There's no turning back now.*

"And," she continued, "I find myself wondering what it would be like to feel those hands and those lips on me."

Anthony was completely taken aback. "Well, now I really don't know what to say."

"I've embarrassed you," Savannah said. "I'm sorry."

"No, no," Anthony was quick to reassure her, "you haven't embarrassed me."

"Then I've made you uncomfortable," she said. "I've put you on the spot, and I didn't mean to do that."

"No." Anthony shook his head. "You have not made me uncomfortable."

She sighed. "Well, then you're going to have to help me out, Anthony. What are you thinking?"

"I'm thinking I can't believe that you feel the same way I do."

Savannah blushed and lowered her head. "You're just being gentlemanly."

"Oh, no." He reached across the table for her hand. As he grasped it, he rubbed his thumb gently across her palm. "I am most certainly not being a gentleman."

Savannah looked deep into his eyes, studying him

closely as if looking for her next course of action in the depths of his almost translucent green eyes. Their eyes locked in a passionate gaze, and then she knew, without a doubt, what was going to come next.

"Can we leave now?" she said softly.

"Yes," Anthony answered quickly. "Yes, we can."

He released her hand, fished out his wallet, and tossed some bills on the table, certainly more than enough to pay their bill and leave a generous tip, apparently not willing to wait for the waiter to bring the check. He rose from his seat and crossed to her side to help her up.

The touch of his hand at her elbow sent small tremors of sensation coursing through her body.

"My place?" His voice was a throaty rumble.

"Yes," she said simply.

It was the last word that would pass between them before they reached his apartment. As he guided his car through the city streets, he held her hand close to his lips, brushing gentle, airy kisses against her skin, both of them wrapped in sweet anticipation.

At his apartment, Anthony held the door for Savannah, and she got her first look at his domain. At some other time, she knew she would take the time to be impressed by the glove-soft leather furniture, the muted charcoal wall color, and the big-screen TV. But now, the furnishings were not the focus of her attention.

Anthony locked the apartment door and turned to face her. "I've never even kissed you," he said. "I've wanted to for a very long time, but I've never done it."

A slow, sultry smile spread across Savannah's face

as she moved closer to him. "Ready to do it now?" she asked.

He pulled her closer to him, wrapping her in the powerful bands of his arms, and laid his mouth to hers.

Savannah felt an instant explosion of sensation from the contact of their lips. And then, Anthony slid his tongue into her mouth, and Savannah thought she would surely faint. In some rational part of her mind that had not been completely consumed by the passion, Savannah reasoned away her reaction to him by reminding herself that it had been nearly a year since a man had touched her like this. But in the soul of her heart, she knew it was more than that. Anthony's kisses had grown more insistent as his hands gently caressed her back and cupped her bottom.

Savannah responded to his passion with an urgency that surprised her. She drew his tongue deeper into her mouth, sucking gently on its moist firmness. Her arms slid around his neck, pulling him even closer. Savannah pressed her body against his and felt the unmistakable evidence of his passion hard against her. His hands continued their odyssey over her body, leaving a trail of fire everywhere he touched her. Their breathing grew more and more ragged as their hearts pounded in throbbing need.

Very soon, the intense kisses were not enough for either of them. Anthony eased her onto the sofa, laying her back against its leather softness, and covered her body with his own. Still fully clothed, they ground their bodies against each other in the age-old ritual of carnal need.

Savannah felt Anthony move away from her

slightly, and opened her eyes to see him staring down at her. Their eyes locked in an intimate gaze. Savannah felt as if she could see into his very soul. To answer the question she saw in his eyes, Savannah gently placed her hands on either side of his face and caressed his smooth skin as she led him back to her mouth. "Yes," she breathed against his lips. *"Please."*

Anthony required no further clearance. He moved into a seated position on the sofa, pulling Savannah up with him. With deliberate, agonizing slowness, he unbuttoned her blouse and planted moist warm kisses on each inch of pecan-colored skin that was revealed as the blouse fell away. Savannah's head fell back and she moaned softly, completely caught up in the silken web of erotic sensuality he wove around her. Once the blouse was gone, Anthony concerned himself with the black lace bra she wore. He lowered his head and nipped gently at her nipples through the fabric. Immediately, Savannah's nipples grew even harder until they were almost painful against her bra. With one deft motion, he released the front closure on the bra and slid it off her shoulders. "You are even more beautiful than I imagined," he whispered. "More beautiful than I dared hope for."

Savannah blushed, unaccustomed to sincere and generous praise. She tugged at the hem of his polo shirt, and he reluctantly pulled back long enough for her to ease it over his head.

Bare-chested, they sat cuddled next to each other on the sofa for a few minutes, exchanging deep, soulful kisses and warm, intimate caresses. Eventually, Savannah stood and faced him as she peeled

away the jeans she was wearing. She watched his face
closely, and was thrilled to see the hunger in his eyes.
In short order, she stood before him naked, warmed
by the heat of his intense gaze. Never breaking eye
contact with her, Anthony quickly unzipped his
pants and maneuvered his hips enough to shed his
pants and briefs. Before he kicked the clothes away,
he fished in the back pocket and retrieved his wallet.
He looked away from Savannah just long enough to
fish a condom packet out of his wallet. Then he
tossed the wallet into the same pile as his pants. She
watched as he tore open the package and quickly
rolled the condom into place.

Still seated, he leaned back against the sofa, his
manhood fully erect and ready, and crooked a finger
at her. "Come here," he said, his voice a throaty
whisper. "Have a seat."

Uncertain of his intentions, Savannah moved to sit
next to him.

"No." He reached for her hips and guided her to
his lap. "Here."

She straddled his lap, and he held on to her hips,
easing her onto his erection. Savannah gasped as he
penetrated her, a gasp that turned into a whimper as
he began to move under her. She laced her fingers
together behind his neck and moved with him, feeling every inch of his shaft as he slid in and out of her
body. When her eyes closed and her head fell back,
Anthony stopped moving.

"No," he commanded. "Look at me."

Savannah raised her head and did as he asked. As
she gazed into his translucent green eyes, she found
herself transfixed, almost in a trance. He began to
move again; this time the intensely intimate stare

they were sharing only served to heighten their awareness of each other so that they were not just bodies but spirits connecting.

Their rhythm matched in passion and need, Savannah and Anthony melded into one body, one soul. Their thrusts grew faster and more insistent, more urgent and more demanding, until Savannah could no longer maintain eye contact.

Surrendering to the orgasmic wave that engulfed her, she threw her head back and screamed his name as she reached her fulfillment. Anthony's peak was close behind. Pushed over the precipice by Savannah's release, Anthony thrust deeply into her and groaned as he felt his hot seed shoot from his body.

It was several minutes before either of them had recovered enough to speak. Savannah buried her face in his neck, overcome by the emotions that bubbled inside her. Anthony pulled her closer to him, until there was no easy way to tell when she ended and he began. They sat that way for several minutes, clinging to each other, neither able to articulate the feelings. Finally, Savannah moved away from his lap and cuddled on the sofa next to him.

She knew that eventually she would have to get dressed and have him take her home, but for right now, all she wanted, all she needed was this man next to her, softly stroking her hair, gently kissing her forehead, and securely holding her next to his heart.

Fifteen

When Savannah awoke the next morning she felt different somehow. As she lay in bed gathering her thoughts, she realized the difference in her life was Anthony. It was so much more than a night of passion, she knew. And she refused to cheapen the experience by trying to rationalize it away.

That man touched my soul in a way it has never been touched before, she thought.

She stretched languorously in her bed and savored the remembered sensation of Anthony's hands and lips and tongue all over her body. Even though she'd made her decision to divorce Dwayne long before she'd made her decision to make love with Anthony, the absolute rightness of her experience with Anthony reaffirmed her conviction about the decision concerning Dwayne.

"I have to take care of this today," she said to herself. "There's no reason to wait any longer."

Savannah decided to call a family meeting to share her plans with her sisters and her children. After another languid stretch, Savannah climbed out of bed and started her day.

* * *

Across town, Anthony was also having a lazy, reflective morning. His experience with Savannah had reached him in places he had thought were inaccessible. He connected with her in a way that shook him with its intensity. When he drove her home after they'd made love, he felt unexpectedly bereft when she got out of his car and left him to go into her house. Even though he knew it was only temporary, even though he knew she would be in his arms again soon, he felt so connected to her that he was unwilling to break that connection, even for a brief period of time.

Anthony shook his head in wonder at how quickly and intensely Savannah Raven Dailey had consumed his life. He didn't quite know what to make of it. It was not something he had been prepared for, not something he had sought. But Anthony knew as surely as he knew that the brightness of spring comes after the gloom of winter that his life would never again be complete without Savannah in it.

He imagined that he should be concerned, maybe even questioning his own sanity, to be feeling this strongly this quickly, but Anthony accepted the absolute rightness of it. He knew, without fully understanding how he knew, that he had reached a turning point in his life.

As he got out of bed, the first thing on his mind was to call Savannah. He needed to know it had been real, not some figment of his passion-addled imagination. Following his heart rather than the conventional wisdom that had men playing it cool on "the morning after," Anthony called her.

"Hello?"

Anthony sighed, feeling the inexplicable rightness

that came whenever he was around Savannah. "Good morning, beautiful."

"Anthony," she breathed. "What a wonderful way to start the morning."

He had no doubt that she meant that as sincerely as he did. "I'm sorry, I know I probably shouldn't have called you this early. But I needed to hear your voice. I needed to know that last night wasn't just a dream."

"Maybe a dream come true," she said softly.

"Savannah, how has this happened so fast?" he asked her, hoping she could give him the explanation that his heart could not. "This time last year, I never even knew you existed, and now I can't imagine existing without you."

"I don't have that answer, Anthony," Savannah said. "And as you know, my life from this time last year until now has been one complete change. And if I've learned nothing over this past year, I've learned that everything happens for a reason. Even if we don't know what that reason is, we have to be prepared to roll with it and move on." She paused briefly. "I don't know what the great cosmic reason for Dwayne's disappearance was. But maybe one of the reasons was to bring you into my life."

Anthony nodded to himself. "That was truly the good in that horrible situation," he agreed.

After a moment of thoughtful silence, Savannah cleared her throat. "I have to go," she said. "I have a lot of things I need to take care of today."

"Can I call you later?" he asked.

"I insist upon it. I'll be waiting to hear from you. Call me at home later tonight."

"I will," Anthony assured her. "I will."

When the call terminated, Anthony was ready to get up and start his day. He sprang out of bed with a whistle on his lips and a lilt to his step that had not been there before.

The best is yet to be, he thought happily.

Savannah gathered her sisters and her children in her family room early that evening. She had insisted that everyone be together "because I'm only going to say this once" she told them. Once the family was assembled, Savannah began.

"There are a couple of things you guys need to know," she said. "And I wanted to tell you as soon as possible. As you all know, I was out of town earlier this week. What you don't know is that I went to New Orleans to see Dwayne."

Various stages of shocked reactions met Savannah's announcement.

"How did it go?" Paris asked.

"How is he?" Stephanie asked.

"When is he coming home?" D.J. demanded.

Savannah raised her hand. "Let me finish. First of all, Dwayne's fine," she said. "He's healthy, apparently happy, and seems to be living quite large." She managed to say that with only the slightest trace of bitterness in her words. "Anthony traced him to a hotel in New Orleans and I went to confront him. I wanted to hear what he had to say."

"Well, what did he say?" Jakarta blurted out.

Savannah chose her next words carefully, knowing that her children hung on every syllable. "He actually didn't say much. He apologized and said he could explain, but he never really did," Savannah said. "We talked for a few moments—"

"Argued more likely," Sydney interjected.

"—and then I left the hotel," Savannah continued, "and flew back home."

"So when is he coming home?" D.J. asked again.

"He's not, son. He's moving on with his life, and now it's time for us to move on with ours."

The finality of the words seemed to penetrate the shield that D.J. had erected around his heart. The stoic mask he tried to wear crumbled, and he began to cry softly. Savannah went to him and cradled his head against her heart.

"It's okay baby," she crooned, "it's okay. We're doing fine without him."

"Will I ever see him again?" Stephanie asked, red-eyed.

"I don't know," Savannah said. "He knows where we are, and he knows how to get in touch with us. Maybe when he's ready, he'll come back around. But for now, I don't think you should look forward to that happening."

In her sisters' eyes, Savannah saw a myriad of questions and she knew that later when the children were not with them she would face a veritable firing squad of sister interrogators. But for the time being, each Raven sister sat silently.

"There's something else," Savannah said. "I have decided to go ahead and file for divorce."

In sharp contrast to the reactions about her trip to New Orleans, no one seemed particularly surprised by her divorce announcement.

"I should think so," Paris said softly.

"I contacted a lawyer today and he has already

begun working on the papers that will need to be filed." Savannah took a deep breath. "I don't know how long it's going to take, but it can't be soon enough for me."

Jakarta, who alone knew that Savannah had not come in until the wee hours of the morning, tilted her head and studied her oldest sister carefully. "Is there something else you want to tell us?" she asked.

Savannah shot her a warning glance.

"Something else like what?" Sydney said. "What else is there?"

"I think Savannah ought to tell you," Jakarta answered.

Paris's brow furrowed. "Tell us what?"

After sitting under the scrutiny of five pairs of expectant eyes for as long as she could stand it, Savannah said, "What Jakarta is not too subtly hinting at is that I went out again last night with Anthony Martin."

"Oh." Paris nodded knowingly. "So how'd that go?"

Savannah paused for a moment as a warm wave of remembered sensation washed over her. "It went fine," she said, fighting to control the goofy smile that was struggling to break out across her face. "But that's not the point here. Whatever happens with Anthony, I would still be getting this divorce. It's time for all of us to move on."

Everyone, even D.J., nodded in understanding.

A short time later, D.J. and Stephanie left the room, leaving the sisters to talk in more intimate detail.

"Come on, give!" Paris said. "What is your relationship with Anthony?"

"Anthony is a wonderful man," Savannah said, "and I'm happy when I'm spending time with him. I don't know what if anything it is beyond that. And rather than jinx it, I think I'll just choose not to talk about it."

"I don't know if that's your choice," Sydney said. " 'Cause I don't know if we're through talking about it."

"Well, go on then, talk about it all you want. I just won't be contributing to the conversation." She gave them a sly smile. "You fill in the blanks however you choose."

"Aw, that's no fun," Jakarta complained. "You know you're supposed to kiss and tell."

"Nothing to tell," Savannah insisted. "Move on." The sisters shared a laugh.

"Well, good for you, Savannah," Paris said finally. "Whatever happens with Anthony, good for you."

Despite her determination to keep her private life private, Savannah couldn't resist a wicked grin. "Oh, yes, it certainly was good for me," she said. "It certainly was."

The sisters' knowing giggles filled the room.

Sixteen

After the family meeting, Savannah felt a sense of peace she had not experienced in nearly a year. She was able to go about her daily routine confident that her life was finally moving in the right direction. The lawyer she'd hired to handle the divorce was following her directive to take care of the legalities as quickly as possible. Because the lawyer was so efficient, Savannah was able to focus her attention on the things that were important to her, her family, her business, and her budding relationship with Anthony. But on one particular day, her past took center stage again.

The light knocking drew Savannah's attention to the door. "Come in," she called, looking up from the paperwork she had spread across her desk to greet her visitor. "Paris! What are you doing here?"

"I was just in the neighborhood and I thought I'd drop by," Paris replied.

"Oh, Paris, that's just a sad excuse. You weren't anywhere near this neighborhood," Savannah chided.

"Okay, so you caught me," Paris admitted. "I wanted to see how you were doing; I knew you were getting the paperwork today."

Savannah looked down at the papers on her desk. "The courier just dropped it off," she said softly.

"Savannah Raven Dailey versus Dwayne Dailey Senior for dissolution of marriage," she read aloud.

"How do you feel about all this?" Paris questioned.

"Oh, it's time. There's no doubt about that," Savannah said firmly. "I am ready to move on to whatever's next in my life."

"Whatever's next?" Paris gave her a sly grin. "Don't you mean 'whoever's' next?"

"I'm not thinking in those terms at all," Savannah said, "and neither should you be. I have to admit though, I'm enjoying Anthony's company quite a bit."

"Why wouldn't you?" Paris said. "He's handsome, young, and successful, and apparently, mad about you. Some girls have all the luck."

Savannah put aside her own concerns to focus on her sister. "It'll happen for you, too, Paris. It will, I promise."

Paris shrugged. "Your mouth to God's ear," she said lightly. "I think about seventy-five pounds away from it happening for me."

"Paris, you are a beautiful, caring, giving woman. It doesn't matter what you weigh."

"Spoken like a sister who loves me," Paris said. "But we are not getting ready to get into my problems now. I came to check on you."

"I'm okay," Savannah assured her. "Trying to prepare myself for what the lawyer tells me may take a while. The lawyers will try to serve Dwayne with the papers at his last known address, but we don't hold out much hope that he's still there. Since we're not sure where he is, they will have to post a notification for him probably in the papers and wait a specified period of time for him to respond."

"What if he doesn't?" Paris asked.

"We're pretty sure he won't, so there is a whole set of steps that have to be taken in order to divorce someone who is not present. The lawyers will take care of most of it for me," Savannah said. "So I'll be able to go on with my life even while this process is going on."

"How are the kids feeling about it?"

"I think they've made their peace with the fact that their father is not coming back. Even D.J. has acknowledged that we all need to move on." Savannah absently tapped a pen against the desktop. "So I'm not going to pretend this is a happy time for them, but they're going to be okay."

"It's been a long road," Paris observed. "Glad to see you all doing so much better."

"All of us, Paris." Savannah reached for her sister's hand and held it firmly. "All of us got through this together."

A knock at the door interrupted them. "Yes, come in," Savannah called.

"I'm looking for Savannah Raven Dailey." The voice belonged to an imposing-looking man in a Detroit police uniform.

Slowly, Savannah rose from her chair and stood behind her desk. "I am Savannah Raven," she said. "How can I help you?"

"Are you the wife of Dwayne Dailey, also known as Randolph Mann?"

Savannah sucked her teeth. "Yeah, that'd be me. But not for much longer."

"Mrs. Dailey, I have some news for you. Did you

know your husband was in New Orleans?" the officer asked.

"Yes." Savannah nodded. "I saw him there a couple of weeks ago. What is this about?"

"Your husband was found dead in New Orleans, Mrs. Dailey."

It was as if the air had been sucked out of the room. Savannah and Paris stared at the police officer in slack-jawed disbelief.

"What are you saying?" Savannah found her voice first. "What happened?"

"All I know is that his body was found in a hotel room about a week ago," the officer answered.

"Oh, my God," Savannah breathed.

"I can't believe it," Paris mumbled.

The officer reached around his back and produced a set of handcuffs. Savannah looked at him dumbly, not registering the significance of the restraints.

"I'm sorry, Mrs. Dailey, but I have orders to place you under arrest." The officer moved toward Savannah's desk.

"What?" The word burst from Savannah's mouth.

"You've been indicted and are to be held downtown pending extradition to New Orleans to face charges in the murder of your husband." The officer grabbed Savannah's unresisting hands and clicked the cuffs around her wrists.

"Indicted? Extradition? There's been some mistake," Savannah mumbled, her senses dulled by the shock of cold steel against her body.

"Savannah Raven Dailey," the officer intoned, "you have the right to remain silent. Anything you say can and will be used against you in a court of law. You have the right to an attorney . . ."

He went on with the recitation of Savannah's rights, but the rest of the words were completely lost on her.

Everything that happened after that was a colorless blur. Savannah was led into the police station and seated next to an old gray desk. The officer who had arrested her asked the standard questions necessary to fill out a police report. Savannah heard a voice she barely recognized as her own mechanically answering.

She moved woodenly through the processing, flinching as the flash from the camera that took her mug shot temporarily blinded her, grimacing as the officer pressed her fingers in ink so he could make a record of her prints.

Before she was fully aware of what had happened, she found herself cold, afraid, and alone in a jail cell. She'd never even visited a jail before, and now unbelievably she was sitting in a cell waiting for the nightmare to end.

I thought I had come out on the other side. I thought it couldn't get any worse than it had been. I thought the worst was behind me. She wrapped her arms around her body, hugging herself, trying to ward off a chill that had very little to do with the actual temperature of the cell.

Her thoughts were a jumbled mass of confusion. *How could this be happening to me?* she wondered. *When I last saw Dwayne, he was very much alive and spitting fire. How could anybody think I had anything to do with his death?*

The starkness of the word pulled her up short.

"His death," she said softly. "Dwayne is dead."

She felt an unexpected sadness engulf her. *I wanted to divorce him,* she thought. *I wanted him out of my life. But I never wanted him dead. What did you do, Dwayne? What kind of life were you leading that wound up with you dead in a hotel room?*

She remembered a time, several months earlier, when she'd wanted to pretend that Dwayne had died, a time when she thought that his dying would be preferable to his abandoning them. But now she realized how very wrong about that she had been. Now, faced with the reality of Dwayne's death, she was feeling overwhelmed by the finality of it all. She allowed pleasant memories of their life together to resurface in her consciousness, memories she had deliberately tamped down ever since his disappearance.

And then she cried. She cried for what should have been, she cried for what would never be again, and she cried for the loss of her children's father—the man who had once been the great love of her life. Her heart ached for D.J. and Stephanie. And even more than she wanted her own freedom, she wished she could hold them and comfort them.

Concerns about her own predicament were temporarily pushed aside by her grief. Sitting on the worn mattress on the concrete slab that served as a bed in the cold loneliness of her jail cell, Savannah grieved.

Eventually, a guard approached her cell. "Savannah Dailey?" the woman said brusquely. Savannah looked up and nodded. "You have a visitor."

The guard unlocked the cell door and directed Savannah to follow. Grateful to be out of the cubicle,

Savannah followed the guard to the visitation room. Her face immediately brightened when she saw Anthony on the other side of the glass.

"Oh, my God, Savannah!" Anthony rushed to the Plexiglas window separating them. "I came as soon as Paris called me."

"Anthony! Thank God you're here," Savannah breathed. "This is crazy. They think I killed Dwayne."

"I know, baby. Paris told me what's going on."

"Anthony, what am I going to do?"

"We'll get you out of here," he promised. "You didn't kill Dwayne, and we're going to find a way to prove that."

"I can't believe this is happening to me." Savannah was incredulous. "You see this kind of stuff in the movies all the time, but it isn't supposed to really happen."

"It's going to be okay, Savannah, I swear to you we're going to get you out of here."

"What about bail?" she asked. "I have some money, and Sydney will put up the rest."

"It's not a bail situation," he said, shaking his head sadly. "They're holding you for an extradition hearing."

"Extradition?"

"Since Dwayne's body was found in New Orleans, they've got jurisdiction over the case. You were indicted in absentia in New Orleans based on whatever evidence they think they have against you. The New Orleans police want you to come there to answer charges, so they have to get a judge to order you extradited to their jurisdiction. The hearing is first thing tomorrow morning."

"Can they do that? Can they just indict me if I'm

not there and then send me to halfway across the country to New Orleans?" Savannah's eyes widened in fear.

"Don't worry, we're going to fight this. We've gotten you an attorney, and he's going to be representing you at the hearing."

"What evidence is it that they have?" Savannah wondered.

"We'll find that out at the hearing," Anthony said. "New Orleans has got to show just cause for you to be sent down there. So we'll be able to hear what 'just cause' they think they have at the extradition hearing."

"Well, they must think they know something," Savannah reasoned. "They wouldn't have gone to all this trouble and expense if they didn't think they had something."

"Them thinking they have something doesn't necessarily mean anything," Anthony tried to reassure her. "Because we have the truth. Whatever they think they have, it's wrong. Because there's no way you killed that man."

Savannah felt strengthened by his confidence in her. "After everything that's happened, having you stand by me is more than I could have hoped for."

"But it's not any less than you deserve," Anthony said.

"Anthony, I don't know what to do. I've never had to face anything like this before."

"You're going to be okay," Anthony insisted. "In the last year you've had to face all kinds of situations you've never had to face before and you've always come out on top. You're going to be okay, and we're going to get through this together." His eyes locked with her eyes in an intense gaze. "I swear to you, I will not rest until this is behind us and your name is cleared."

"Thank you so much," Savannah said. "It means more to me than you can imagine to have you on my side."

"Where else would I be?" Anthony smiled at her.

"Unless you're her lawyer, it's time for you to leave," the female guard interrupted them.

Reluctantly, Anthony nodded. "Okay, I'm going. Savannah, I'm going to get right on this. Paris asked me to tell you that she and your sisters will be taking care of things at home. We'll see you tomorrow at the hearing. Try not to worry."

Tears began to well up in Savannah's eyes. "I don't know how I got so lucky to have so many wonderful people around me. I love you all."

Anthony felt a warm glow having been included in the accounting of people Savannah loved. After one last encouraging smile, he left the jail and immediately headed back to his office.

"Since Savannah didn't kill Dwayne, the key is to figure out who did," he said to himself. "Maybe there's some information that I overlooked in the file."

He was anxious to get to his office to go through the Dailey file and try to uncover Dwayne's killer.

Seventeen

"What are you saying?" D.J. screamed at his aunts. "Dad's dead?"

Jakarta reached out to the boy. "I would give anything if this weren't true. But it is, baby. The New Orleans police found your father's body in a hotel room."

As soon as the police took Savannah from her office, Paris had sprung into action. Her first move was to call Anthony and apprise him of the situation. She knew that he would rush to the jail to be with Savannah. Her second call was to Sydney, but her sister was in a meeting out of the office and could not be reached. After leaving an urgent message on her voice mail, Paris bolted out of the Dailey Plumbing office and made a beeline for Savannah's house. The kids weren't home from school yet, so Paris had a few minutes to brief Jakarta on the situation. Together, the sisters were fighting their own shock to help the children through theirs.

"And they're saying Momma did it?" Stephanie's voice was barely a hushed whisper. "That's not possible."

"We know that, sweetie," Paris reassured her. "But until we can prove that, they're going to keep your mother in jail."

"Oh, no, it can't be." Stephanie curled up in a ball on the sofa, sobbing uncontrollably. "Daddy can't be dead . . ." She repeated the words until they were almost a mantra. Paris rushed to be by her side, rubbing the girl's back and shoulders in an effort to soothe her.

D.J. stood stoically silent, his face an emotionless mask.

"Talk to me, D.J.," Jakarta urged.

D.J. shook his head for a moment before responding. "I knew Daddy had to be dead," D.J. said finally. "Because if he wasn't dead, he'd have been here. He'd have come back."

Jakarta shook her head sadly. "D.J., you believe whatever you need to believe. But right now, your mother needs your strength. You know she didn't have anything to do with this, don't you?"

D.J. looked away from his aunt's intense scrutiny.

"Answer me," Jakarta demanded. "Tell me that you know your mother didn't have anything to do with your father's death." Jakarta grabbed the boy by his upper arms and shook him.

"I know, I know," he yelled finally. "I know she wouldn't do anything like that. It wouldn't matter how mad she got or how hurt she was, Momma is just not the kind of person who could do something like this."

Jakarta almost cried with relief. She pulled her nephew closer to her and hugged him fiercely.

"What's going to happen to Mom?" Stephanie managed through her tears.

"Your mother is going to be fine," Paris said emphatically. "Anthony Martin, that detective that was working with us before, is back on the case. He's going to find the evidence we need to clear your mother's name. It's all going to be okay, I promise."

Stephanie seemed to take some comfort in her aunt's words. But she still visibly mourned the loss of her father.

"My daddy's dead," she sobbed quietly. "My daddy's dead . . ."

By the time of the extradition hearing the next morning, Savannah was a nervous wreck, having slept barely at all in the cell. She was led into the courtroom, shackled in a line with several other female prisoners who were due in court that day. As she filed into the courtroom, she looked around for her family and was immediately relieved to see them all there. Jakarta had brought the children, a move that Savannah wasn't completely convinced was wise, but she had to admit, she was very, very happy to see her children there. But the one face that lifted her spirits the most was Anthony's. He sat at the end of the row next to Paris and smiled encouragingly at Savannah. Just his strong presence was enough to calm her nerves a bit.

She sat through the proceedings, watching as several women faced the judge before her. All too soon, her turn came. She took her seat at the defendant's table next to the attorney Anthony and her sisters had hired.

"It's okay," he assured her in a whisper, "this is only an extradition hearing; this is not the trial."

"But this is where they decide whether or not to send me to New Orleans, right?"

"Yes," the attorney said, "but even if that happens, it's not the end of the line."

"Even if that happens?" Savannah gave him a shocked look. "It sounds like you've given up already."

The lawyer never got a chance to reply because the judge called for Savannah and her accusers to stand and face the court.

"John Tyler for the defense, Your Honor."

"Zane Reeves, assistant prosecutor, New Orleans, Louisiana, Your Honor."

Savannah stole a look at the New Orleans prosecutor and was struck by his apparent youthfulness. *What is he, sixteen?* she thought caustically.

"Welcome to Detroit, Mr. Reeves," the judge said.

"Thank you, Your Honor," Zane Reeves replied.

"So what have you got?" the judge asked.

"Your Honor, the city of New Orleans requests that Savannah Raven Dailey be extradited to our jurisdiction to answer charges in the murder of her husband, Dwayne Dailey, also known as Randolph Mann." Reeves spoke quickly and efficiently.

"What evidence do you have to support this claim?" the judge asked.

"Mrs. Dailey is known to have a motive, having been abandoned by her husband several months earlier," Reeves said, consulting a legal pad on the table in front of him. "We have evidence that Mrs. Dailey was in New Orleans at the time of the murder. We have witnesses who put Mrs. Dailey at the crime scene and who observed Mr. and Mrs. Dailey in a heated argument in the lobby of the hotel where the body was discovered. These witnesses will testify that she was the last person seen with him before his body was discovered."

"What about the murder weapon?" Savannah's attorney injected. "Do they have the murder weapon?"

"What about it, Mr. Reeves?" the judge asked. "Has the murder weapon been recovered?"

"Not yet, Your Honor, but the police are looking for it and expect to have it soon."

"I see." The judge made notes on his pad.

"How can they bind her over for trial without a murder weapon?" Savannah's attorney demanded.

"Good question, Mr. Tyler," the judge, said, nodding, "but that will be a decision for the trial judge to handle. As you know, for our purposes here they only need to show just cause." The judge turned to the prosecutor. "I'm going to rule in your favor, Mr. Reeves. I believe you have shown enough evidence to warrant the extradition. I am going to order Savannah Raven Dailey immediately extradited to New Orleans to face charges." He banged his gavel. "Next case."

"No, Mommy!" Savannah heard Stephanie cry out. Savannah turned and reached out for her daughter but was quickly restrained by the courtroom guards. The last thing she saw as she was led away was the shocked, saddened expressions on the faces of her supporters.

So, I'm going back to New Orleans, was the only coherent thought she could manage.

When Savannah was led out of the courtroom, pandemonium erupted among her family.

"How can this be?" Jakarta demanded. "She's innocent."

"This is not justice," Paris yelled.

Anthony was quick to herd them out of the court-room and into the hall.

"What do we do now?" Sydney asked him. Savan-nah's family looked to Anthony for answers.

"I guess we're going to New Orleans," he said. "But everybody doesn't need to go. I'll go and re-port back to you."

Jakarta shook her head. "I'm coming with you. One of us needs to be there for Savannah."

Paris nodded. "I agree. I'll stay at the house with the children. You go on to New Orleans with An-thony."

Sydney reached into her purse and pulled out a credit card. "I'll pay for your trips," she said. "And your hotel while you're there. Go and be with her. Make sure she's not alone."

Jakarta nodded her understanding. Just as she and Anthony were preparing to leave the courthouse, Jakarta saw the New Orleans prosecutor exiting the courtroom door. She hurried over to him.

"How could you?" she demanded. "My sister is innocent. How could you?"

"If your sister is innocent, we'll find that out once we get her to New Orleans." Zane gave her a look and marched on.

Jakarta glared at his departing back. "I'll see you in New Orleans," she said.

Eighteen

Later that same day as she was being processed for transfer to New Orleans, Savannah kept telling herself, "It's just another jail cell, and it's just a matter of time before I'm outta here anyway. I know I didn't kill Dwayne and soon the court will know I didn't kill Dwayne too."

But all of her rational thinking did nothing to help her face the reality of being sent to New Orleans to jail. She was escorted to New Orleans by the youthful prosecutor Zane Reeves and a heavily armed marshal. Silently, she suffered the humiliation of being led through the airport in handcuffs, the subject of curious stares and unkind whispers. She was marched past her fellow passengers to be seated first in the back of the plane. She refused to acknowledge either the prosecutor or the marshal as she was directed to the middle seat and squeezed between them on the plane. But as the plane took off and they flew south, she discovered she could hold her tongue no longer.

"You know I didn't have anything to do with Dwayne's death." She addressed Zane. "I was divorcing him," she said. "The court courier had just delivered the divorce papers the day you had me arrested. Why would I be divorcing him if I had killed him?"

Zane shrugged his shoulders. "I don't pretend to fully understand the motives of the people I prosecute," he said shortly, "but if I had killed a spouse and was trying to cover my tracks, filing for divorce would be an excellent way to do that, wouldn't you think?"

Savannah huffed in indignation. "You are all wrong about this. While you are spending New Orleans's money trying to nail this on me, somewhere out there a killer is running free."

"Time will tell, Mrs. Dailey, time will tell." He fell silent, and, frustrated, so did Savannah.

When they arrived in New Orleans, they were met by a prisoner transport van. And even though Savannah was the only prisoner being transported this day, she had to sit in the back of the van, chained to her seat, a steel cage separating her from the driver.

Prosecutor Reeves sat in front with the driver as they transported her to the jail.

"This doesn't seem like overkill to you?" she said to the backs of the men's heads. "You've got me chained up here like I'm some kind of mass murderer or something."

Zane half turned in the seat to face her. "Frankly, Mrs. Dailey, we do think you're a murderer," he said. "You've been brought to New Orleans to face murder charges. This is standard procedure under these circumstances."

"I did not kill my husband," Savannah hissed at him. "You have to know that."

"So you've said. By the way, that's what they all say, Mrs. Dailey." Zane turned back to face the front.

Frustrated, Savannah pulled at her restraints. "You're treating me like some kind of animal. This is ridiculous!"

"The ride's almost over, ma'am." The marshal spoke for the first time. "We'll be there shortly; you should try to relax."

Savannah sat back against the hard, cold seat, resigned to the fact that there was nothing she could do.

When they reached the jailhouse, a guard came out to meet the van. Savannah watched as paperwork was signed, transferring her from the marshal's care to the jailer's care.

Just like some kind of parcel they had to deliver, Savannah thought caustically.

Zane shook hands with the marshal. "Thanks for your help," Zane said. "The trip went very smoothly."

"No problem," the marshal replied. "See you next time."

Zane left the jailhouse without acknowledging Savannah's presence.

I am not used to being treated like this, Savannah thought. *I am not a criminal.*

She followed the guard through the corridors to the processing center. It all seemed very surreal to her. As she went through the frighteningly familiar motions of having her mug shot taken and her fingerprints recorded, Savannah deliberately detached herself from the action.

This is not my life, she repeatedly said to herself. *Not my life.*

* * *

Jakarta and Anthony reached New Orleans a few hours after Savannah did. Their first stop directly from the airport was the parish jail where Savannah was being held. Once they discovered she was only allowed one visitor at a time, Anthony encouraged Jakarta to go visit her sister.

"I want to check in with this prosecutor Reeves," he said, his jaw set in a hard line. "I want to know what it is he thinks he knows."

Jakarta nodded. "Good luck, Anthony."

After agreeing to meet up at the hotel later, they parted company and went on their assigned tasks.

Zane Reeves was conflicted. He usually had a gut instinct about his cases and in the time he'd been serving the people of New Orleans, he'd come to trust his gut. Now his gut was screaming at him that Savannah Raven Dailey was not what she appeared. On paper, based on the evidence that had been gathered, it had seemed obvious to him that Savannah Dailey killed her husband, most likely in a fit of passionate rage. But having spent the time with her during her transfer to New Orleans, he now was beginning to have doubts about that assessment. And it wasn't just that she seemed like a nice lady, he thought. It was that she seemed utterly stunned at having been charged with this crime. No twinges of guilt or looks of smug superiority or fear at having been caught flitted across her face. Zane had seen only confusion and outrage. Both of which were consistent with people who had been wrongfully accused. Zane was weighing his gut versus his evidence when a knock on his office door interrupted him. "Yes?" he said.

Anthony stood in the doorway. "Mr. Reeves, my name is Anthony Martin and I'm a private detective from Detroit," he introduced himself. "I wondered if you might have a few minutes to speak with me about the Dailey case."

Zane looked up from his desk and stood to meet Anthony eye-to-eye. "Since you're a private detective," he said, "surely you know that I can't get into the specifics of this case with you."

Anthony nodded. "I do understand that. But I would still like a few minutes of your time. Even if you can't get into specifics with me, maybe you could listen to what I have to say."

Zane shrugged and motioned for Anthony to come in and have a seat. "Sure, I've got a few minutes," he said. The men settled into their chairs.

"Mr. Reeves, you've spent time with Savannah on the flight here, I know," Anthony began.

Zane nodded.

"Does she strike you as a killer?" Anthony asked.

"Mr. Martin," Zane said, "it has been my experience that the best killers never do seem to be killers."

"I understand that," Anthony said, "but the case you have against her is circumstantial at best. And I know you know she was divorcing him."

"Yes, Mrs. Dailey pointed that out on the plane," Zane said dryly. "And as I pointed out to her, if one was trying to cover one's tracks after having killed a spouse, filing for divorce might be the smartest way to do that."

"Believe me, that would require a level of guile and deceptiveness that Savannah Dailey is just not capable of," Anthony asserted.

Zane leaned back in his chair and steepled his fingertips under his chin. "What's your connection to this case, Mr. Martin?" he asked.

Anthony hesitated for a moment, formulating his answer. "I was hired by the Dailey family to track down Dwayne Dailey after his disappearance. I can tell you without any doubt, that Savannah Dailey was not interested in finding him. She had decided to let him go on his way."

"Well, at some point she changed her mind," Zane pointed out, "because she showed up in New Orleans. There's no question about that."

"Yes," Anthony agreed, "but she'd come down here to try to get some answers from him, to try and understand why he would abandon her and their children." Anthony took a deep breath. "Savannah Dailey is a highly respected businesswoman. She has two teenaged children and everything in the world to live for. Her life has improved tenfold since Dwayne Dailey left. Why would she ruin all that now?"

"Crimes of passion are almost never rational," Zane said.

Anthony felt his frustration growing. "At least tell me what you have on her," he asked.

Zane furrowed his brow. "Why is it so important to you, Mr. Martin?"

"Savannah Dailey is a very good friend of mine," Anthony said. "And I know she has been wrongfully accused."

They sat silently, each man taking the measure of the other.

"I shouldn't be doing this," Zane said after a long moment.

"But you understand why it's important that you do." Anthony radiated intensity.

After studying Anthony closely, Zane suddenly understood why this Detroit detective had taken such a personal interest in this case. "Okay, I get it," Zane said softly.

"So are you going to tell me?" Anthony asked.

Zane reached into a drawer in his desk and pulled out a file. He laid the file in the center of his desk and rose to go. "If you'll excuse me, Mr. Martin, there is some business I have to attend to with my secretary. I'll be back in about twenty minutes." He gave Anthony a look that spoke volumes and then left the office.

As soon as the door closed behind the prosecutor, Anthony reached for the file that Zane had left on his desk. As he suspected, it was Savannah's file. Anthony pored over the details of the case against her. He made quick mental notes about the material that the New Orleans police had gathered. By the time Zane Reeves had returned from his "business," Anthony was finished.

The prosecutor entered the room and resumed his seat. "Now, where were we, Mr. Martin?"

"I think we're finished here, Mr. Reeves." Anthony stood to leave. "I understand the predicament you're in. Thank you for your time," Anthony said, genuinely grateful, as he left the office.

* * *

At the county jail where Savannah was being held, Jakarta had to wait for what seemed to be an interminable amount of time while Savannah was processed before she was allowed to see her sister. Finally, a guard led Jakarta to a small cubicle with a Plexiglas window. She sat in the hard metal chair and waited for her sister to arrive.

"Jakarta?" Savannah was shocked to see her. "What are you doing here?"

"The family decided that I would come to New Orleans to be with you so you won't be alone down here."

"But who's with the children?" Savannah asked.

"Paris is going to stay at your house until you get home. Don't worry," Jakarta assured her, "we've got it all covered."

"Until I get home . . ." Savannah's voice trailed off. "Jakarta, I'm scared."

Jakarta nodded. "I know, sis, but don't be. Anthony's here in New Orleans too, and he's doing everything he can to get you out of this."

"Anthony's here?" Savannah felt a small kernel of hope form in her gut. "Where is he?"

"They would only let one of us see you at a time, so he went to talk to that cocky prosecutor Zane Reeves." Jakarta practically spat the name. "Anthony was hoping to get some information from the guy. He told me to tell you he would see you later."

Savannah nodded. "How long are you staying in New Orleans, J?" Savannah asked.

"I'm prepared to stay here as long as I need to. We've all talked about it and decided we couldn't leave you down here by yourself."

"Thank you," Savannah managed through her tears. "Thank you so much."

They talked for a few more minutes, and then a guard approached Jakarta, telling her her time was up.

"I'll be back tomorrow, sis," Jakarta promised. "Hang in there, we're all with you."

Savannah smiled weakly, wanting to put on a brave face, and watched as her sister left. With a heavy heart, Savannah followed the guard back to her cell. She tried to think up some comforting words that might give her peace, but she had no luck.

I don't know if I'm going to be able to handle this much longer. She climbed onto her bunk, pulled the pillow over her head, and began to cry softly.

When they met up at the hotel later that day, Anthony and Jakarta compared notes. Anthony briefly told her about his meeting with the prosecutor.

"He let me see the case file," Anthony said, "and their case is pretty much circumstantial. I've been thinking about it all day, and I think the truth we need to get Savannah off is not here in New Orleans."

Jakarta nodded. "You think you need to go back to Detroit?"

"I have considered the possibility that Dwayne's killing was a random attack, but the New Orleans police would not have gone all the way up to Detroit to get Savannah if they thought it was some local druggie who'd done this. Furthermore, the evidence that Reeves let me see indicated that Dwayne knew his killer. There had not been a forced entry into the hotel room and there were no apparent signs of a struggle. So it seems unlikely that Dwayne was killed by a random act of violence." Anthony clenched and unclenched his fist unconsciously as he pieced the case together.

"If all that's true, that means that somebody other than me had to have been looking for Dwayne and had to have found him at about the same time."

"Why?" Jakarta looked confused.

"Otherwise, the killer would have gotten to Dwayne at one of those other places he visited," Anthony reasoned. "And if Dwayne's killer was someone he knew, it was possibly someone from Detroit."

"It sounds like your choice is clear," Jakarta said. "I know you don't want to go, but—"

"But I will serve her cause better if I'm back on my own stomping grounds and working my own sources," Anthony said reluctantly.

"Then you need to go back to Detroit." Jakarta was firm. "I'll stay here with Savannah. She won't be alone."

Anthony nodded. "I'll take a flight out tomorrow afternoon, after I've seen Savannah."

As Anthony waited in the visitors' area for Savannah to be led in from her cell, he wondered what he would say to her to explain his decision to return to Detroit. He wanted to make sure she knew that he was not abandoning her, not now and not ever. The stress of the ordeal was starting to take its toll on Savannah. Her hair was unkempt, and the gray jumpsuit she'd been issued hung off her body like a burlap sack. Her face was drawn and haggard; her normally rich pecan-colored skin was pale and dry. But the stress truly showed in her eyes. Red and puffy from crying, her eyes' vacant, lost look revealed the turmoil churning in her soul.

"Oh, baby," he breathed, at a loss for words when she appeared. "Savannah, darling, how are you?"

"I'm scared, Anthony," she answered honestly. "I didn't kill Dwayne, but that doesn't seem to matter. I keep thinking about every story I've ever heard about people who were wrongfully tried and convicted and wound up spending the best years of their lives in jail for a crime they didn't commit. What if that happens to me?"

"It won't happen to you, because I won't let it." Anthony's voice was strong and firm. "I'm going to get you out of this. You have to believe that."

Savannah hung her head. "I think I have to prepare myself for the worst," she said.

"No!" Anthony's response was quick. "You have to have faith, believe in the system"—she made a face—"and if you can't believe in the system, believe in me. Savannah, look at me."

With an effort, she lifted her eyes to meet his.

"I swear to you, I will not rest until I have proven your innocence."

Their eyes stayed locked on each other for several long moments, Savannah drawing strength from Anthony.

"I'm going back to Detroit today," he said finally. "I have some new information that I got from the prosecutor here and I believe I can track down some evidence in Detroit."

"You're leaving?" Savannah whispered.

"But I'm coming back," he assured her. "And

when I do, it'll be to take you home. I give you my word. Do you trust me?"

Savannah managed a nod. "With my life," she said simply.

Before he left New Orleans, Anthony placed one last call to Zane Reeves.

"Mr. Reeves, this is Anthony Martin."

"Yes, Mr. Martin?" Zane sounded slightly annoyed.

"I just called to tell you that I'm leaving town today."

"Oh, you've had enough of visiting our fair city?"

"I'll be back," Anthony assured him, "but my investigation will go faster if I'm back home in Detroit. I want you to have my phone numbers in Detroit so if anything turns up, you'll know where to reach me."

"I don't think I need that information," Zane said. "If there's any new information, Mrs. Dailey's attorney will know, or it will come out in court."

Anthony nodded to himself. "Okay, but let me give you my numbers just in case." He began to recite the numbers slowly, certain that even though he professed not to need them, Zane was making note of them.

"Thank you again for your help, Mr. Reeves," Anthony said. "I will be in touch."

"Have a safe journey back to Detroit, Mr. Martin," Zane said noncommittally.

Anthony went to the airport, confident that he had a friend in Zane Reeves.

Nineteen

Once he returned to Detroit, Anthony attacked his task of finding evidence to clear Savannah like a man possessed. He retraced the steps he'd made in his initial search for Dwayne. But this time, he had a new focus. Before, he had just been trying to find Dwayne. Now he was trying to find out *about* Dwayne. He needed to know everything Dwayne did and everywhere Dwayne had been, and everyone Dwayne knew, because somewhere in that mix he was certain there was a killer. It was a new slant on the investigation for him.

Anthony focused all his energies and all his resources on Savannah's case, making it a priority over all his other work. He knew he would not rest until she was cleared of all charges.

Anthony interviewed people who hadn't seemed necessary to talk to before, and reinterviewed those who had. He checked out leads and tips he received, and slowly a totally different picture of Dwayne Dailey emerged.

Dwayne, it seemed, was something of a ladies' man. Anthony discovered the names of four women with whom Dwayne allegedly had affairs. Two of the affairs seemed to have happened at approximately the same time. Dwayne had been lavish with gifts for these women and had maintained an apartment across town from his home for his trysts.

Anthony was frustrated and more than a little embarrassed that he hadn't turned up this information before. But now that Dwayne was dead, people seemed more willing to talk more openly about him. The Dwayne Dailey file Anthony had was growing.

He was sitting in his office listening to a tape of a recent interview with one of Dwayne's mistresses when the phone rang. He answered the phone on the second ring.

"Martin Investigations, Anthony Martin speaking."

"Mr. Martin, this is Zane Reeves in New Orleans."

"Mr. Reeves." Anthony sat up at attention. "Has something happened?"

"I really shouldn't be calling you to tell you this," Zane Reeves began.

"And you already know how much I appreciate the fact that you are," Anthony said. "What is it? What's happened?"

"The police recovered the murder weapon," Zane said.

"Well, that's excellent news," Anthony said. "Since Savannah's fingerprints didn't match the ones on the gun, you're ready to let her go—right?"

"Not so fast, Martin," Zane said. "There were no fingerprints. The officers recovered the gun in the canal."

"Damn!" Anthony swore.

"But ballistics tests confirm that this gun was definitely the murder weapon. So that's a good thing. And someone tried to remove the serial number and did a really shoddy job of it, because it was only halfway done. A partial serial number was recovered on the weapon."

"Go on," Anthony said.

"You realize I shouldn't be making this call," Zane said again.

"I know that, and so did you when you decided to pick up the phone," Anthony said. "And I also know that you know how much I appreciate it. So come on, what's the number?"

After a brief pause, Zane read off the numbers. Anthony quickly jotted them down.

"Thank you, Reeves. You don't know how much this means to me."

"I think I do," Zane answered. "Good luck, Martin." The call was terminated.

Anthony was thrilled by this new development. He realized if he could track down the gun's owner, he would probably have found Dwayne's killer. He switched on his computer and accessed a police data bank of gun registration numbers and began his search.

After an exhaustive search of the different possible combinations of serial numbers, Anthony had narrowed the field to ten potential weapons that could have killed Dwayne. His next step would be to try and locate those weapons. Any that were missing or not accounted for would become the prime suspects.

It was tiring work, and Anthony had been at it continuously since receiving the call from Zane Reeves. The numbers were starting to swim before his eyes, and he knew intellectually that he was tired and needed to take a break, but his heart wouldn't let him.

He stopped long enough for a cup of coffee and was about to resume his number checking when Sydney Raven entered his office.

"Hi, Anthony," she said tentatively, "I hope this isn't a bad time."

Anthony rose to greet her. "Sydney, this is a surprise. Have a seat. What brings you down here?"

She settled into one of the wing chairs positioned in front of his desk. "Well," she said, "I feel so helpless with what Savannah's going through. Paris is looking after the kids, Jakarta is in New Orleans so Savannah won't be alone, you are digging around trying to find any and everything you can to clear her. It just feels like there's something I ought to be doing."

Anthony nodded. "I know this is a terribly difficult time for everybody."

"So," Sydney continued, "I came in to see if there was something I could do to help you? Put me to work; I'm ready and willing to help."

Anthony leaned back in his chair and studied her closely. "Actually, Sydney," he said, "there really isn't anything you can do to help me."

"Well, what are you working on?" she asked. "Tell me what the status is."

"I got a break in the case—some new evidence surfaced recently. Zane Reeves, the prosecutor in New Orleans, called me to say the gun that was used to murder Dwayne had been recovered."

That's good news, isn't it?" Sydney said hopefully. "I mean, now we know Savannah didn't do it. Her fingerprints wouldn't have been on the gun."

Anthony shook his head. "It is good news, but it's not definitive. There were no fingerprints on the gun; it was recovered in water. What they did find was a partial serial number. I was able to get that from Reeves, and now I'm cross-referencing it against registered guns to see if I can track it down."

"I can help with that," Sydney offered. "Sounds like tedious work. You could use a hand, right?"

"No, actually you can't. But, Sydney, if you really want to help, somebody needs to be looking after Dailey Plumbing."

"I have been keeping the books," Sydney protested. "I've been trying to keep on top of the business's financial health."

"But haven't you been doing that from your office across town?" Anthony asked. "You haven't been down to the shop at all, have you?"

Sydney reared back in her chair as if she'd been struck. "Oh, I don't think I'm going to be able to do that," she stammered. "What good would it do for me to go into the shop? I don't know anything about the plumbing business."

Anthony smiled slightly. "Well, I can't imagine you know much about the gun identification business, and yet here you are volunteering to help."

She nodded, conceding his point. "But honestly, Anthony," she persisted, "the day-to-day operation of Savannah's business is just not something I could do."

"I'm not sure I understand why." He looked at her curiously.

"I don't know anything about plumbing."

"You wouldn't necessarily have to know anything about plumbing," he said. "Savannah has a shop foreman or someone there who knows the plumbing part of it. They'll just need someone to keep them all on task and keep the financial records together. That's what your sister is most worried about."

Sydney didn't answer.

"And she knows that Paris is with the children," Anthony continued. "So she's afraid that with everything that has happened, her arrest could signal the end of Dailey Plumbing."

"But they're *plumbers,*" Sydney burst out finally. "I don't see myself being able to work with plumbers. Frankly, I've never understood how Savannah could do it."

Anthony cocked his head at her. "Sydney," he chided, "you aren't being a snob, now, are you?"

"I don't think so," she said. "And I don't think you ought to be talking to me like that."

"Let me tell you what I don't think, Sydney. I don't think in this time of crisis that it's asking too much for Savannah's family to each step in and do their part. I don't think, in this time of crisis, that it's an unreasonable thing to expect each of us to step outside of our normal routines." Anthony's tone brooked no further discussion. "Savannah told me once that she had always admired your business savvy. She was very impressed by your accomplishments in your field. I know she would love it if you took care of the business for her." He rose to signal the end of their meeting. "You asked me how you can help, and I've told you how you can help. Now if you'll excuse me, I've got some guns to track down."

Sydney stared at him in shocked indignation. She stood up and prepared to go. "You're impertinent," she said haughtily, "but you do have a point." She turned to go, but turned back to face him as a thought occurred to her. "Savannah said she admired my business savvy?" she asked.

"Yes," Anthony answered. "She is very proud of you."

Sydney nodded. "Well, I'll see what I can do," she said as she left.

"You do that, Sydney," he said to her retreating back. "You do that."

Once she was gone, he returned to his task, more determined than ever to free Savannah as quickly as possible.

Twenty

After her conversation with Anthony, Sydney found herself in need of a second opinion. Even though classes would still be in session, she went to Paris's school to talk it over with her sister. When she arrived, Paris was in the middle of an English lesson. Sydney knocked on the glass window of the heavy wooden door. When Paris saw her sister at the door, her face registered her surprise.

"Class, would you excuse me for a minute?" Paris went to the door and stepped out into the hall.

"Sydney!" She hugged her sister. "What on earth are you doing here?"

"I need to talk to you, Paris. I need your thoughts about something." Sydney nodded toward the class. "I guess now is a bad time?"

"Give me twenty minutes; then they'll be going to lunch and we can talk." Paris opened the door. "Come on in and have a seat in the back." Sydney followed Paris into the classroom. The buzz of conversation that had started in her absence silenced immediately when Paris returned.

"Class, I'd like you to meet my sister, Sydney Raven," Paris announced.

"Hello, Miss Raven," twenty-two fourth graders chimed in unison.

"Uh, hi, everybody." Sydney felt very much on display. She moved to the back of the classroom and slid into one of the few empty chairs.

"Now where were we?" Paris resumed her lesson. For the next twenty minutes, Sydney had a refresher course on subject-verb agreement. By the time the class filed out for lunch, Sydney was impressed.

"You're really good with those kids, Miss Raven." Sydney smiled. "I don't know how you do it."

"It's not that big a deal. I really enjoy the kids, and I love the moment when they get it. It's almost like I can see the lightbulb go on above their heads." Paris stacked some papers on her desk. "But that's not why you came here in the middle of the day, so suppose you tell me what's on your mind?"

Sydney moved to the front of the room and sat directly across from Paris's desk. "I went to see Anthony earlier, and he gave me something to think about."

"So tell me. Does it have something to do with Savannah's case?"

"No, not exactly." Sydney took a deep breath. "Ever since Savannah's arrest, Dailey Plumbing has been running more or less on its own. I've been taking care of the books, but the day-to-day operation of the business has been left to the employees."

Paris nodded. "Yes, I know all that. What's this got to do with Anthony?"

"I'd gone to see Anthony to offer to help him with his investigation on Savannah's case. He told me there wasn't anything I could do to help him with the case, but then he said if I really wanted to help, I should go and see about Dailey Plumbing. He said Savannah is worried about the business surviving."

"So what's the problem, Syd?" Paris studied her closely. "Anthony's right, the business does need some personal attention. I think that was an excellent suggestion he gave you."

Sydney gave her sister a pleading look. "But, Paris, they're plumbers! And the shop has to be dirty and smelly . . . it's just not something I'm comfortable with."

"Sydney!" Paris's tone was full of reproach.

"Look, Paris, I am what I am. And what I am is a woman used to a little class, style, and refinement. I just don't see myself spending my days in a workshop surrounded by plumbers." Sydney reared back in the seat and folded her arms across her chest.

Paris's face was a disapproving mask. "So why have you come here? What did you want me to say? That's it's okay for you to let Savannah's business go down the tubes because you're too good to work with plumbers? If that's what you're after, then sorry, Syd, I can't help you."

Sydney didn't respond for a long moment. "Actually," she said finally, "I am a little ashamed of myself for having let the business go unattended for so long. I guess phone reports from the staff are not going to be enough." She tossed her head, whipping a stray piece of hair out of her eyes. "But in my defense, I never thought Savannah would be away this long. I really believed the whole situation would be cleared up in a matter of days."

"Well, now that it hasn't, all of us have to step up and help out," Paris said firmly. "And you are the only one who can take care of the business." A sly grin appeared on Paris's face. "You're just going to have to get over your aversion to plumbers."

"Yeah, okay," Sydney conceded. "I'll go to the shop in the morning. But I don't have to like it."

"Of course you don't, honey," Paris's tone was slightly condescending. "Of course you don't."

The next morning, when Sydney parked her BMW in the parking lot at Dailey Plumbing at a time that she had thought was early, she was surprised to see several cars already there.

"It's only nine. What time do these guys start working?" she wondered aloud.

She entered the shop tentatively looking for the shop foreman who had assumed the lead role in the operations of Dailey Plumbing. As she walked into the shop, she felt ridiculously overdressed. She'd come dressed in the clothes she would be wearing into her own office later that day, but the high-heeled pumps and peach-colored Chanel suit were wildly inappropriate in the plumbing shop. Several of the men stopped their work to look up at her.

"I'm looking for Paul," she said loudly.

"Paul Sims or Paul Jordan?" one of the men asked.

Sydney stood silently for a moment, a perplexed look on her face as she suddenly realized that despite the number of phone conversations she'd had with the man, she didn't know Paul's last name.

"Uh, Paul the shop foreman?" she answered lamely.

"That's Jordan," the answer came. "He's in the back in the welding shop." The man pointed toward the rear of the building.

Sydney nodded and headed in the direction she'd

been pointed. When she reached the welding shop, she saw a tall man wearing a welding mask, using an acetylene torch to cut through a length of pipe. Sparks shot off of the pipe and created a fiery spray where he was working.

"Paul?" Sydney called.

When the man didn't acknowledge that he'd heard her, Sydney took a few steps closer. "Paul Jordan?" she called again.

He turned off the torch and lifted the welder's mask, revealing a man Sydney estimated to be in his late forties. "I'm Paul. How can I help you?"

"I'm Sydney Raven; we've talked on the phone a few times."

"Oh, sure, Sydney," Paul said cheerfully. "It's nice to finally meet you. You know, put a face to the voice." He pulled the thick welding glove off of his hand and extended it for Sydney to shake.

Sydney hesitated for the briefest of seconds, looking at his hand as if inspecting it for dirt before she returned the gesture. If Paul noticed her hesitation he made no comment about it.

"What brings you down here?" he asked.

"My family and I felt like somebody needed to be here to check on how things were going since Savannah's absence has turned out to be longer than we expected."

Paul looked offended. "So what? You don't think I'm doing a good job for Mrs. Dailey?"

"No, no, it's not that at all," Sydney said, immediately trying to smooth the ruffled feathers, "it's just that we didn't think it was fair to put the whole responsibility on you. We felt like someone from the family should be here to help."

"And how are you going to help?" Paul looked her up and down, noting the expensive suit and shoes. "Should I fire up one of these torches for you?"

"I wanted to check in and see how things were going here," Sydney said impatiently. "And you need to remember that you are just an employee in this business."

"Is that so?" Paul said. "Would you like to fire me, and then run this business without me?"

For an instant, Sydney was tempted to do just that. "I don't like your attitude, Paul. You act like I'm some kind of intrusion here, but this is my sister's business and I've come to make sure it's going okay."

"This is my livelihood, Ms. Raven," Paul said defensively. "Without this shop, I don't have a job. So I'm going to make sure it goes okay too."

"Well, then we shouldn't be arguing, because we have the same goal," Sydney said in a haughty tone. "Now suppose you brief me on what's been happening around here."

"Brief you?" Paul looked annoyed. "Yeah, whatever."

"We should go to my sister's office for this conversation," Sydney said.

"Whatever you say." Paul peeled off the protective gear he had been working in and gestured toward the door. "After you."

Sydney paused for a second as she realized that she wasn't exactly sure where the office was.

"Um . . ." she began.

"Yeah, okay, after me then," Paul said sarcastically. He turned and stalked out of the welding shop.

When they reached Savannah's office, Paul moved toward the chair behind the desk.

"Where are you going?" Sydney asked. "I'll sit there."

"Lady, those little power plays might go over well downtown in the big corporate buildings where folks wear two-hundred-dollar shoes to work, but here in this shop, we're all about getting the work done. We don't have time for that kind of nonsense." Paul gave her a scathing look. "I don't care who sits in this chair. But the fact that you do tells me something—I'm not sure what yet—about who you are." Paul stepped off to the side and made a grand gesture to the chair. "Please, have a seat."

Sydney glared at him as she moved to sit behind the desk. "So tell me what's going on around here," she said.

Paul sat in a chair facing the desk and leaned back. "We're filling our plumbing contracts to the best of our ability. I've had a few guys leave because they don't believe the business is going to be able to keep supporting them, so they decided to bail, but I still have some very dedicated men who are working very hard here."

"Well, I've been checking the books," Sydney said, "and there are a few customers who haven't paid yet."

Paul shook his head. "I'm not very good at being a collections agent. I'd much rather just do the work. You know you want to believe that people will honor their commitments, but since I started dealing with the business end and not just the plumbing end, I've discovered that ain't always the case."

"So listen." Sydney leaned forward and put her

elbows on the desk. "It seems to me that both of our skills are needed to keep this business afloat. My sister will be cleared of these charges soon, I'm confident of that."

"Me, too," Paul quickly agreed. "All the guys who have stuck around here know that Mrs. D did not kill her husband."

Sydney smiled gratefully at him. "Thank you for that support. I want to make sure that when this ordeal is over and Savannah comes home, she has a strong, vital business to come home to."

"I agree," Paul said.

"So here's what I'm proposing," Sydney said. "I know we got off on the wrong foot. That was my fault, and I apologize. But if you will agree to keep the jobs going, do the plumbing part of it, I'll take some time off work and come in here on a daily basis to take care of the paperwork side of it."

Paul nodded. "Okay, that's a deal."

This time, Sydney extended her hand to shake. "A deal it is." The two of them clasped hands firmly, sealing their arrangement.

That evening, Sydney joined Paris, D.J., and Stephanie for dinner at Savannah's home.

"So you went to the shop today?" Paris asked as she set a plate of fried chicken on the table.

"Yes, and it went better than I expected," Sydney answered. "Paul is really doing good work over there. But he admitted he was absolutely overwhelmed by the business side of it. So he and I agreed that I would come in and help with the business and paperwork and he would stay on top of the plumbing part."

"So you're going to be going in on a regular basis?"

"I took a leave of absence from my job—they can make it without me for a while." Sydney spooned a bit of tossed salad onto her plate. "And until Savannah gets home, I'm just going to stay there at the shop to make sure she has a business to come back to."

"How long do we think that's going to be, Aunt Sydney?" Stephanie asked. "When do we think Mom's coming home?"

Sydney shook her head. "I don't know, honey. I haven't heard any new information from New Orleans." She turned to Paris. "Have you heard anything?"

"No." Paris shook her head. "The last time I talked to Jakarta, things were still pretty much at a standstill. Anthony is working on some leads, but so far there's nothing concrete to report."

"So she could be there indefinitely, right?" D.J. said.

"No, don't think that," Paris said. "Your mom's going to be coming home soon. She's innocent, and innocent people don't go to jail."

D.J. snorted at that. "Yeah, right. Especially not innocent black people, right, Aunt Paris?"

"You have to believe in the system, D.J.," Paris insisted. "It's all we have. Listen, I have an idea." Paris quickly changed the subject. "Let's write to your mother. I know she'd love to hear from us."

Stephanie agreed immediately. "That's a great idea, Aunt Paris." She sprang up from her seat at the dinner table and went to her room to get paper and pens. While she was gone, Sydney turned to Paris.

"Oh, I don't know about this. What would I have to say?"

"What do you mean what would you say?" Paris was stunned. "Your sister is in jail, for goodness' sake. Tell her you love her, tell her you have her back, tell her that the business is going to be fine. Any encouragement or words from home are better than nothing."

D.J. rose from the table. "May I be excused please?"

"So you're not going to write your mother?" Paris asked.

"Just tell her I said hi," D.J. responded. "That's good enough." He left the dining room.

"It's almost like he's mad at her," Sydney observed. "Do you think he thinks she killed his father?"

"No, I don't believe it's that," Paris said. "I don't even know if he knows why he's angry. He's feeling abandoned—first by Dwayne and now by Savannah, and he's a sixteen-year-old guy. He doesn't know how to handle those feelings."

"Don't you think we should have insisted that he write his mother?" Sydney asked.

"No, I don't think that would do anybody any good," Paris said. "Let him go. He'll come around in his own time."

Sydney made a face. "So why does he get his own time but I have to write a letter?"

Paris silenced her with a look. "Sydney . . ." Her voice had a warning.

"Yeah, okay," Sydney huffed.

By then, Stephanie had returned with paper and pens. "Where'd D.J. go?"

"Maybe he went to do some homework," Paris offered.

"He's not going to write Mom, is he?"

"He's just not ready yet, baby," Paris said gently.

Stephanie sighed. "I wish he'd get over it and support Mom more than this."

"Give him some time; he'll come around," Paris assured her.

Stephanie shrugged and passed out paper to her aunts. "I think it's really cool that we're getting to spend so much time with you again, Aunt Sydney. I really like having you guys here with me. It makes me feel like part of a family again."

Sydney smiled at her niece and reached out to hold her hand. "I'm really glad to be here too, sweetie. I guess I didn't realize how much I was missing my family. But it sure is great to be back in the fold."

"You've always sort of existed on the fringes of the fold," Paris pointed out. "But I agree, this is a good thing. Now if we could just get Savannah and Jakarta home, everything will be better than ever."

The three of them turned to their task of letter writing, a pleasant camaraderie in the air.

Twenty-one

New Orleans Assistant District Attorney Zane Reeves reexamined the Dailey file that sat in the center of his desk. He was becoming more and more convinced that the evidence that had been gathered against Savannah Raven Dailey was circumstantial at best. After his conversation with the Detroit detective, Zane Reeves doubted even more that he had the right perpetrator in custody.

"But," he said aloud, "my hands are tied for now."

"What does that mean?"

He looked up, startled at the voice, and was even more startled to see Jakarta Raven standing in his doorway.

"What are you doing here?" he asked. "You should not be here."

"Don't be ridiculous," Jakarta said dismissively, "where else would I be?"

"Look, Ms. Raven," he said, "we have had this conversation before. There is nothing that I can do for you."

"That's not true." Jakarta came into his office and sat down. "You can authorize the release of my sister. You're the one who has the power to do that, right?"

"Yes, I do have the power to do that," he agreed,

"but while I don't know how things are done in Detroit, here in New Orleans, we tend not to just set murderers free to run the streets without a really good reason."

"So you've made up your mind—she's a murderer? We don't even get the benefit of 'accused' anymore, right?" Jakarta snapped.

Zane sighed and rubbed his brow. "Ms. Raven, I have not made up my mind, and obviously your sister will be given a chance to defend herself. But there's nothing else I can do right now."

"You know she didn't do this," Jakarta said. "I can see it in your eyes."

"What are you talking about?"

"When we first met," she said, "you had such a look of righteousness about you. You had no doubt that you had nabbed this dangerous criminal and made the streets of New Orleans safe again." She studied him closely. "But now as I look at you, I can see you're not sure anymore. Are you?"

Zane automatically glanced down at the file that lay spread out on his desk. Jakarta noticed the shift of his eyes and saw the file that he had been studying. She noticed the bold-print word *Dailey* written on the file label.

"See, I'm right," she persisted. "You are questioning her guilt. You know she didn't kill that man. Why won't you let her go?"

"I can't just let her go!" Zane spoke each word with slow, firm deliberation. "A gut feeling that she didn't do it is not enough of a reason."

"Aha!" Jakarta pounced on his words. "You do know she didn't do it."

"I didn't say that," Zane said quickly.

"Yes, you did," Jakarta insisted. "You know she's innocent. What do we have to do to get her out of here?"

"There is not enough evidence yet for me to consider dropping the charges."

"Yet?" Jakarta questioned. "What does that mean?"

"It means, Ms. Raven"—Zane stood, signaling the end of the meeting—"that I believe the system works. And if your sister is as innocent as you profess, that will be borne out soon enough. Now if you'll excuse me, I have work to do."

"This isn't the end of this, Mr. Reeves," Jakarta promised. "You have not seen the last of me."

"Of that," Zane Reeves said as he held open the door to his office, "I have no doubt. Good afternoon, Ms. Raven."

Jakarta hesitated, not quite ready to be dismissed. She gave him one last stern look, and then disappeared from his office.

Zane breathed a sigh of relief after Jakarta left. He suspected she was absolutely right in her declaration of her sister's innocence. But his hands were tied unless something new was revealed. "Good luck, Mr. Martin," he said softly, thinking about the Detroit detective. "I hope you're as good as I've heard."

Anthony was deeply involved in checking out the ten possible matches for the gun serial number Zane Reeves had given him. For the moment, none of his other cases mattered. He knew there were other things that needed his attention, but he could no more have focused on them than he could have cut out his own heart. Anthony's sole and driving priority was proving Savannah's innocence. It hurt his heart to remember her as he'd last seen her in the gray jumpsuit with *New Orleans Department of Corrections* stenciled on the back, her eyes red-rimmed and panic-stricken. He knew that even if it cost him business and clients, there was no way he would be doing anything else but working on this until Savannah was out of that jail and back in Detroit with her family.

"And me," he said aloud. "I want her back here with me. It's taken me this long in my life to find someone like Savannah, and I won't lose her now."

Jakarta signed in, had her ID checked, and waited in the glass-walled cubicle where Savannah would join her soon. After a few moments, Savannah, dressed in a prison-issue gray jumpsuit, emerged from behind a heavy metal door and took her seat in the chair across from Jakarta. A thick sheet of Plexiglas separated them, making the phone mounted in the cubicle the only way they could talk.

"Hey, sis," Jakarta said into the phone. "How ya holding up?"

"I guess I'm doing as well as I could expect." Savannah's reply was strained. "I've got to be honest, J. I don't know how much more of this I can take."

"Hang in there, sis. Anthony's working overtime trying to find out anything he can that will help."

Savannah sighed tiredly. "Tell me, how are the kids?"

"I talked to Paris this morning," Jakarta said. "And they're okay. Don't worry about the kids. You are the focus right now."

"Why is this happening to me, Jakarta? I don't understand any of it."

"I can't answer that, honey. I can only tell you that there are a bunch of people doing everything they can to get you out of this."

Teary-eyed, Savannah nodded.

"I talked to that prosecutor today," Jakarta said. "He is being incredibly stubborn."

"What do you mean?"

"He's just so unreasonable. He won't even consider any other suspects. As far as he is concerned, the case has been solved."

"He said that?" Savannah looked frightened.

"Oh, I'm sorry," Jakarta quickly apologized. "I shouldn't have upset you like that. Don't worry. I don't care what Mr. Righteous thinks, this is not over . . . not by a long shot."

A guard approached Jakarta. "You're going to have to leave now. Her attorney is here to see her."

Jakarta nodded. "Did you hear that, sis? Your attorney is here—maybe he's got some good news for you."

"Let's hope so," Savannah mumbled. "I'll see you tomorrow?"

"Count on it," Jakarta said firmly.

After Jakarta left, Savannah was led to the counsel room where she would meet with her attorney. Unlike the regular visitation cubicles, the counsel room was open, with no glass between attorney and client. Once the guard opened the door, Savannah took a seat at one of the four chairs placed around the long table. She folded her arms across her body and leaned back against the chair to wait. From the counsel room window, she could see brilliant sunlight, even though it was filtered by the steel cage mesh placed against the windows.

Savannah's attorney entered the room in a rush. "I'm sorry if I kept you waiting," he apologized.

"Hey, I've got nothing but time on my hands," Savannah said flippantly.

The attorney was New Orleans–based and had been recommended by the Detroit attorney her sisters had hired. The Detroit attorney had been unable to come to New Orleans to defend Savannah, so she found herself in the hands of Justin Korrell, a young black man with a baby face and an air of urgency around him.

"I'm afraid I've got some bad news," Justin said. "I've spoken with the prosecutors and they feel like their case is pretty solid."

"But my previous attorney told me the case was all circumstantial." Savannah took a deep breath to try and chase away the panic that threatened.

Justin nodded. "Well, it is basically, but they believe you have the clearest motive and the most opportunity, and sometimes that's really all they need to go forward." Justin took a deep breath, apparently steadying himself for what he was about to say.

"The prosecutors want to offer you a deal. Plead guilty to manslaughter and they'll recommend fifteen to twenty with an eligibility for parole in seven years."

"Are you nuts? What are you saying to me?" Savannah's voice rose. "Does the fact that I didn't kill Dwayne not matter here? That all that matters is circumstance?"

"What matters is our ability to prove that you

didn't kill Dwayne," Justin said. "And right now, we would have some trouble doing that."

"I thought I was innocent until proven guilty," Savannah pointed out.

"Yes," Justin agreed, "the burden of proof is on the state. But they believe that they can make that burden, so much so that I've been told if we refuse the deal, they're going to go ahead with murder one."

"Doesn't that mean premeditated? And doesn't that carry the death penalty?" Savannah's eyes widened with fear.

Justin's nod was slow but definitive.

"Let me get this straight." Savannah got out of the chair and began pacing in the small space. "Either I admit to something I didn't do and agree to go to jail for a minimum of seven years, or I go on trial— for something I didn't do—and risk being sent to the electric chair." She stopped in her pacing to glare at the young attorney. "Is that pretty much my choice?" She waited for his confirmation.

"That pretty much sums it up," Justin said. "What should I tell them?"

Savannah's glare changed to a look of incredulity. "Tell them I didn't do it!" she snapped. "And tell them there's no way I'm going to admit that I did!"

Justin nodded his approval. "I expected that would be your response, but I'm obligated to bring you all offers, no matter how ridiculous they are."

"Yeah, thanks," Savannah said sarcastically. "So, you got any more news for me?"

"I've been in contact with your detective in Detroit, and he has some new information that he's working on. He wanted me to let you know that he's working very hard on the case."

Savannah smiled slightly. "Well, that's good news at least. What about bail? Don't I get a chance to post bail? Can they just hold me here until the trial?"

Justin shook his head. "They convened a grand jury and indicted you before you even got down here," he said. "And then they used the indictment to get the extradition order. So as far as the New Orleans system is concerned, you are a dangerous murderer and a flight risk. I've requested a bail hearing, but the wheels of the system are moving very slowly these days. And frankly, even if we got the hearing, I'm pretty certain bail would be refused for you, since you're from out of town and have no local ties."

"So I'm just stuck here," Savannah said, "here in this box until they either convict me and send me to the penitentiary, or until there's enough evidence to clear me. Is that basically what you're telling me?"

Justin Korrell looked pained, but he was forced to agree. "I'm afraid so." He opened his briefcase and pulled out a small packet of letters. "I do have some good news for you. I have some mail for you from your family. They sent it to me so it would get to you directly." He slid the letters across the table to her.

"This is the best thing you've said to me since you've been here," she said. "Thank you." She picked the letters up and rose from the table. "I expect you'll come back if anything changes."

"Try not to worry too much, Savannah. We are all working very hard to prove your innocence."

"Somehow," she said caustically, "that doesn't comfort me very much right now." She banged on the door, calling for the guard. "Guess I'll just go on back to my luxury suite, and read my mail."

As Savannah returned to her cell, somewhere in the recesses of her humanity she realized she had been hard on the young attorney. Intellectually she knew he was doing the best he could under a difficult set of circumstances. But emotionally, she was not prepared to concede that.

Once she entered her cell with her letters clutched in her hand, her cellmate looked up. When Savannah first arrived at the New Orleans jail, she was put in a community cell with a dozen other female prisoners. That holding cell had been temporary. Within the first couple of days, Savannah had been assigned a two-inmate cell, sharing space with a prisoner named Ginger, a forty-something repeat offender with dyed red hair and a tough, show-no-mercy exterior.

"Back already, Newbie?" Ginger looked up from the magazine she had been reading. "Usually these visits of yours last longer."

Savannah sighed and rolled her eyes. "Ginger, why do you insist on calling me that?" she asked. "I have told you half a dozen times, my name is Savannah."

"I don't like that name," Ginger said dismissively, "and Newbie very clearly explains who you are. It's so obvious you don't know anything about this place or this system."

"And what are you, the old pro?" Savannah said.

"I've got a little experience under my belt, and I remember my first time and how scared I was." Ginger rolled up into a seated position on her cot. "I'm just trying to help you out, Newbie."

"Well, then I'll say thank you and leave it alone." Savannah gave up trying to get Ginger to address her correctly.

"Looks like your visit didn't go very well today. Did your attorney come by?"

"Yeah, he came," Savannah grumbled, "for all the good it did me. The only news he had was an offer from the prosecutor to plead guilty for a so-called lesser penalty."

"I'm guessing you're not interested in that, huh?" Ginger asked.

Savannah shot her a fiery look. "Of course I'm not interested. I didn't do it! I didn't kill my husband."

"Yeah." Ginger nodded knowingly. "That's what matters in here."

Savannah chose to ignore the comment, not wanting to get into a debate with Ginger about the peculiarities of the justice system.

"He did have some letters for me from my family," Savannah said, changing the subject.

"Cool." Ginger nodded. "At least you got that. My kids gave up on me a long time ago. I don't ever hear from them anymore."

"How old are your children, Ginger?"

Ginger laughed shortly. "My 'children' are twenty-four, twenty-two, and nineteen—two boys and a girl. They're through with their old mom. Can't even count on them to bail me out anymore."

Savannah shook her head. "That's terrible."

"Well, I try not to judge them too harshly," Ginger said. "I've been in and out of this place and places like it so many times, they're just tired. I'm tired, too."

"Look, Ginger, I don't know what you did—we've

never talked about that and I'm not asking now—but whatever you did, if you're tired, can't you stop?"

"Sounds like it would work on paper, don't it, Newbie?" Ginger laughed ruefully. "But it hasn't seemed to go that way. I don't know, maybe there's something addictive about this place—once you get here, you just like it and want to come back again and again."

"I don't think so," Savannah said. "I'm counting the days until I can get out of here."

"So you think they're gonna let you go, huh, Newbie?"

"I didn't do it; I didn't kill my husband," Savannah said yet again. "That's got to count for something."

"You would think so, wouldn't you?" Ginger gave her a sage look. "Go on, Newbie, read your letters. They'll bring you some comfort. Lord knows there's precious little of that to be found around here." She picked up her magazine and returned her attention to it.

Savannah settled on her bunk and untied the ribbon around the package of envelopes the attorney had given her. On the top was a letter from Stephanie. Savannah recognized her handwriting right away. Under that was a letter with Paris's handwriting on it. The third envelope had a typed address from Sydney. Savannah figured Paris had made Sydney write it. Noticeably absent was any correspondence from D.J. That absence hurt Savannah's heart.

He must be so upset about all this, she thought. Remembering Ginger's words, Savannah said a brief prayer that D.J. would not abandon her the way Ginger's kids had discarded their mother.

She turned to her letters. Stephanie's letter was chatty and lighthearted, filled with news of the trials and tribulations of an eighth grader. Paris's letter was reassuring, filled with good news about the children and how much they missed her. Paris made a point to include news of D.J. in her letter.

> *He's doing pretty good, sis. It's a tough time for him like it is for all of us, but he's spending time with his friends and keeping up with his schoolwork. He just needs you to come home—like we all do.*

Savannah smiled at that news. Sydney's letter had information about the business and how she was handling the challenges of Dailey Plumbing.

> *I swear, Savannah, this is so much more involved than I ever thought. Who knew plumbing was such a complicated business? That Paul guy you have at the shop has been a godsend. He has really helped me out, being a go-between for me and the crew. And when you get home, we're going to talk about cleaning that shop up.*

Sydney had closed that sentence with a little happy face. *Hurry home, sis, we love you and we miss you.*

"I have got to get out of here," Savannah muttered.

"What's that, Newbie?" Ginger looked up from her magazine.

"I don't know how much more of this I can take," Savannah said. "I didn't do it. Why should I have to keep sitting here?"

"Well, Newbie, the wheels of justice can turn a

little slow. But there are other ways to get out of here."

Savannah's eyes narrowed. "What are you talking about?"

"Come on, Newbie, you've seen enough movies, you know what I'm talking about." Ginger cast a sideways glance at her.

"A jail break?"

"Shhh!" Ginger immediately silenced her. "The walls have ears, Newbie. Just know that if you ever really get fed up, there might be another way."

Savannah shook her head. "I'm innocent, and I'm not making any more trouble for myself by doing something stupid."

Ginger shrugged. "Just wanted you to know you've got options."

Savannah rolled her eyes and began to reread her letters. *Please, Anthony,* she thought, *please get me out of here.*

Twenty-two

Anthony was getting excited. His serial number checking had narrowed ten numbers down to three of the most likely candidates for the murder weapon. All three of the guns he was focusing on had been purchased in the Detroit area. He couldn't be sure, but his instincts told him that Dwayne's killer had been a local enemy.

He checked his watch and was stunned to discover it was well past one A.M. "Damn," he muttered. "Too late to contact the gun shops." Resigned to the fact that the next step would have to wait until the next day, Anthony turned off his office lights and prepared to go home.

"It's almost over, baby," he promised an absent Savannah. "If this goes like I hope it will tomorrow, you'll only have a few more nights in that jail."

He left the office to go home and grab whatever snatches of sleep he could until the morning when the gun shops would open and he could continue his search.

The next day started with Anthony making the rounds of the gun shops. The guns had been purchased in three different shops—two of the owners he knew, one he didn't. It was going to take some guile to coax the name out of the shop owner he didn't know, but Anthony was a determined man.

At the first two shops, owned by people he knew, the task was easy. The owners willingly gave Anthony the names and addresses for the two guns purchased there. The third shop owner was not so quick to surrender the information.

"Do you have a search warrant?" the owner asked.

"I can get one very easily," Anthony bluffed. "This gun may have been used in the commission of a murder. I'm sure you don't want to interfere with a murder investigation."

The owner stood his ground.

"Look, make this easy for yourself. If I have to go get a search warrant and come back, I'm going to be pissed, and I'll most likely have to tear the whole place up looking for your records." Anthony leaned on the counter. "I just need one name and I'm outta here and you won't have to worry about seeing me again."

The owner hesitated a bit, clearly considering.

"One name . . ." Anthony urged.

Finally, the owner relented. He went to the back of the shop and returned with a thick ledger book. "What did you say that serial number was?"

Once Anthony had all the names matched with the gun serial numbers, he hurried back to his office to check them out. Two of the names meant nothing to him and generated no connection in his mind. But the third name, Kent Julian, connected with him for some reason he couldn't quite put his finger on.

"Kent Julian." He said the name again, rolled it over in his mind, and tried to remember why it sounded so familiar. He flipped through the pages of the Dailey file, focusing on the new information he'd recently uncovered about Dwayne's secret life.

"Oh, my God, could this be it?" Anthony's eyes were riveted to a name he'd found as one of Dwayne's mistresses. "Anna Julian? Could she possibly be related to Kent?"

The possible connection was too tantalizing to ignore. Anthony flipped on his computer and opened a database that would allow him to cross-reference the names. He entered the name Kent Julian, and immediately a screen of vital statistics on the man popped up. One entry jumped off the computer screen at him and caused his heart to leap into his throat.

"Spouse," he read, "Anna Julian." He leaned back in his chair and let the full import of the entry resonate with him.

"This gun that may have killed Dwayne is registered to Kent Julian, who is the husband of one of Dwayne's girlfriends." Anthony connected the dots. "Oh, my God."

He whirled around in his desk chair, snatched the phone off its hook, and immediately placed a call to New Orleans.

"Zane Reeves." The call was answered on the second ring.

"Reeves, this is Anthony Martin. I've found it."

"Found what?" Zane was curious.

"I've been checking those serial numbers, and to make a long story short, there's a gun that has a comparable serial number that is registered to a man named Kent Julian who lives here in Detroit. Kent

Julian is the husband of a woman who had an affair with Dwayne Dailey."

"That is intriguing," Zane encouraged him, "but it doesn't change anything."

"How could it not change anything?" Anthony demanded.

"You don't have enough information," Zane told him. "You don't know if this Julian's gun is missing, you don't know if he was ever even in New Orleans. There's just not enough information. But it sounds like you're going the right way."

"Okay, I understand," Anthony said. "I will keep digging . . . I'll find the truth." Anthony hung up the phone and leaned back in his chair. The biographical information about Kent Julian was still displayed on his computer screen. As he looked back at it, he saw another entry that sent chills down his spine.

Place of employment: Dailey Plumbing.

"What?" Anthony breathed. He immediately turned to the file and flipped through the papers until he found an employee list. He ran his finger down the list, stopping at the entry for Kent Julian. He scrolled across the list and noticed the termination date. He remembered that day. *That was the day Savannah had to lay off some of her employees.* Kent Julian had recently been laid off from Dailey Plumbing.

"Sounds like a man with a motive," Anthony said grimly. Convinced that he had found Dwayne's killer, Anthony made note of Julian's address and planned to go there to confront him. Realizing that he would need proof, he pondered for a moment, considering the best course of action. He reached into a drawer and retrieved a small microphone and tape recorder.

I'll wear this wire when I meet with Julian. He paused, thinking. *If I'm right, this Julian is a killer,* Anthony realized. *Maybe just a microphone and tape recorder is not going to be enough protection.*

Anthony reached for the phone and called in a favor.

"Fifth Precinct, Sergeant Robinson speaking."

"Chuck," Anthony said, "I need your help."

"What's up, Tony?"

"I'm on a case, and I'm about to confront a possible killer. I need you to have my back."

"Shouldn't you leave confronting killers to the police?" Chuck asked.

"Trust me, this is something I have to do. Can you cover my back?"

"I've always got your back, Tony. When and where?"

Anthony gave his friend the address and the men agreed upon a time.

If you did this, Julian, Anthony swore, *I will get you.*

In New Orleans, Zane Reeves was fast becoming backed up against the wall. His superiors were pressuring him to bring the Dailey case to trial. His boss felt it was bad for tourism for murders in elegant hotels to go unprosecuted. But the more Zane heard from Anthony, the more convinced he became that Savannah was not the killer. Zane was stalling, trying to give Anthony time to prove Savannah's innocence before the start of a trial. Zane knew that once a trial started, it would be harder to release Savannah if Anthony turned up new evidence. The plea offer had been one of Zane's stalling techniques. He knew that if she was innocent there was no way Savannah Dailey would accept the plea, but just putting it on the table bought Zane—and Anthony—a little time. Zane was mulling over the significance of his most recent phone call from Anthony—a new suspect— when his boss walked in.

"Reeves, what is the status of the Dailey case?" County Prosecutor Samuel Duvall demanded.

"And hello to you, too, Sam." Zane's tone was sarcastic. "Come on in and have a seat."

"Don't be funny, Reeves," Sam said as he entered the office and settled into a chair. "Just tell me what's going on with the Dailey case."

Zane shrugged. "You know the status. Mrs. Dailey turned down the plea. So I guess we're going to trial."

"And when will that be?" Sam demanded. "Are you even on the court's docket yet?"

"Um . . . I'm not sure," Zane stalled. "I will check and see. You know how full the docket is these days. It can take a while."

Sam shook his head. "No, I want this fast-tracked. The people of New Orleans, and more importantly the guests of New Orleans, need to know that our hotels and streets are safe."

Zane studied him curiously. "And how, exactly, will fast-tracking this trial accomplish that? I'm not sure I'm clear on that point."

"Look, Reeves." Sam's impatience showed. "Once we prove that this man was murdered by his es-tranged wife, then it becomes a crime that could have happened in any city. It's not a random act of violence and it's not related to the safety of New Orleans. If the murder was between intimates, and

especially intimates from out of town, then its being
in New Orleans becomes incidental. So we need to
get this handled as soon as possible to ease the public's mind."

Zane displayed a look of intense concentration. "I
didn't know the public was worried about this," he
said.

Sam rose from his chair. "Look, just do it. Get the
case on the docket and get it taken care of. The
evidence is clear from what I've seen. There's no
reason this should take very long."

"It really hasn't been that long," Zane pointed
out. "But I will do what I can."

Sam nodded curtly and turned to the door. "Oh,
by the way"—he turned back to face Zane—"the
police who are investigating this case tell me that
someone else apparently is checking into the same
evidence."

"Oh?" Zane tried to appear unconcerned.

"Yeah, the gun serial numbers," Sam said. "The
police tell me that someone else has accessed the
police database. Checked into those same numbers.
You wouldn't know anything about that, would
you?" he asked.

Zane shrugged. "The police database must be a
huge thing. I can't imagine that it's that rare to have
more than one person accessing numbers." Zane
looked annoyed by the whole line of questioning.

"Uh-huh." Sam was unconvinced. "Just let me say
this, I don't think I have to tell you that you should
not be having any contact with the defense team.
That could create some problems down the road."

"We're all looking for the same thing," Zane

pointed out. "We're all after the truth. Whether we are prosecutors or defense attorneys."

"Or private detectives from Detroit," Sam inserted.

Zane shrugged. "We're all looking for the same thing and I don't think it should matter who gets to it first."

"We already have the truth," Sam said. "We know who killed that man. Now let's close the books on this one." Sam paused for a moment, locking eyes with Zane. "You were assigned this high-profile case because somebody thought it would help your career," Sam continued. "Don't blow it now."

"It's under control, Sam," Zane assured him.

With a nod, Sam left the office.

Zane took a deep breath. "Better hurry, Martin," he said quietly.

Twenty-three

At the appointed hour, Anthony and his police officer friend met across the street from Kent Julian's modest house. Anthony had already outfitted himself with the microphone, concealed under his clothes. He handed his friend a receiver box.

"You'll be able to hear me on this, Chuck," he said.

"You sure about this, Tony?" Chuck asked again. "I can go on in and get him if you want."

"We don't have any grounds for you to go in and get him," Anthony pointed out. "I don't want this guy slipping away on a technicality. If he did what I think he did, he needs to be thoroughly nailed to the wall."

"Okay, I'll be right out here listening," Chuck said. "And be careful."

Anthony went to the front door of the Julian home and knocked. He knocked several times and was about to give up when the door was finally snatched open.

"What!" a man growled.

Anthony looked the man over from top to bottom. He had obviously been drinking, and from the looks of him, had been drinking for quite some time. "Are you Kent Julian?"

"Who wants to know?" the man asked.

Anthony produced a badge from his pocket. "My name is Anthony Martin and I'm a private detective. I wonder if I might talk to you for a few minutes."

"I don't have anything to say." Kent tried to close the door.

Anthony blocked the door with his body. "It will only take a few minutes. Is Mrs. Julian home? I'd like to talk with her, too."

At that, Kent snorted. "There is no Mrs. Julian," he said, "not anymore."

"Oh? What happened?" Anthony said.

"Not that it's any of your damn business," Kent said, "but Mrs. Julian decided to leave me in search of greener pastures." Kent took a deep draw from a beer bottle he had in his hand. "Fat lot of good that did her," he mumbled bitterly.

"Mr. Julian, I am investigating the death of Dwayne Dailey." Anthony watched closely to see if there was a change in Julian's demeanor. "I'd like to talk to you about your gun."

"M—my gun?" Kent stammered. "What gun?"

"I happen to know you own a thirty-eight-caliber revolver that you purchased at Global Guns five months ago," Anthony said icily. "Incidentally, a thirty-eight caliber was used to kill Dwayne Dailey, so I wondered if I might see your gun please."

"Um, I don't know where it is right now." Kent's eyes darted around the room. "Maybe that bitch Anna took it with her when she left." Kent's face changed as he spoke. "Yeah, that's it. Maybe Anna shot that bastard in the face after he dumped her." Kent nodded vigorously. "Yeah, that's who you should be looking for . . . Anna."

"What makes you think so?" Anthony questioned.

Kent took another swig from the bottle. " 'Cause it all makes sense. Anna and Dailey had been messin' around for a long time and she left me and ran off with him. But then he dumped her—seems Dailey never had any intention of marrying Anna." Kent seemed to warm to the story he was telling. "Guess that's what set her off, Anna, I mean. She must have tracked him down to New Orleans and busted a cap off in his ass."

Anthony could no longer contain his disgust for the man. "You're a damn liar . . . and a lousy one at that."

"What are you talking about?"

"Your wife did not kill Dwayne Dailey. We both know that. What kind of man blames a woman for something he did?"

Kent glared angrily at Anthony.

"You want to know how I know you did it?" Anthony moved closer to him. "I never said anything about Dailey being shot in the face or being shot in New Orleans, but somehow you knew both of those details. How is that?"

Suddenly Kent turned on his heel, threw the beer bottle against the wall, and bolted to the back of the house. Anthony was caught flat-footed as the suspected killer ran through the kitchen and out the back door.

"Damn!" Anthony swore. "He's on the move, Chuck," Anthony yelled into the microphone as he took off after him.

Anthony caught sight of Kent turning a corner into the alley that ran along the back of his property. Anthony ran with all the speed he could muster, chasing after him. Anthony saw Kent run into the street and heard the squeal of tires and the blares of horns as traffic skidded to a halt to avoid hitting the desperate man. Anthony was close on his heels, running through the streets. For at least two blocks, the men ran down the center of the street, sticking to the yellow line as if it were the road to Oz.

"Where are you, Chuck?" Anthony huffed into the microphone. "We're heading south on Marshall Street. Cut him off!"

A car that Anthony recognized to be Chuck's swerved and screeched to a halt broadside in Kent's path.

"Stop! Police!" Chuck jumped out of the car screaming.

Rather than stopping, Kent made an abrupt left-hand turn and ran in the opposite direction. That slight delay was enough to allow Anthony, who had been gaining on him, to reach him. Anthony dove at the man's ankles, tackling Kent and pulling him to the ground. They crashed against the asphalt, knocking the breath out of Kent, and bashing Anthony's chin against the ground. Anthony felt the sting of the cut on his chin and saw blood begin to darken the ground near him, but he held on to Kent Julian's legs. Kent struggled against Anthony's hold, but was unable to break away.

"If anybody ever deserved to die it was Dwayne Dailey." Kent spat the words. "He took everything from me . . . my wife . . . my job . . . my dignity." He tried to kick again. "I say the world is better off without him."

"Chill, Julian," Anthony instructed. "Don't make this situation any worse than it already is." Anthony righted himself and yanked Kent's hands behind his back, holding him there until Chuck arrived with the handcuffs.

Unexpectedly, Kent laughed harshly. "Make the situation worse? Hell, man, that's the story of my life! My life just keeps going from bad to worse. I'll tell you what though, one of the best things I ever did was kill that bastard Dailey. You don't know the satisfaction I felt when I shot that smug look off his face."

Kent stopped struggling against Anthony's restraining hold as he got caught up in his memories. "It took me a while to find him—or should I say it took you a while to find him." Kent twisted around to look harshly at Anthony. "But as soon as Mrs. D. took off to New Orleans, I knew that's where he'd be. I followed her to that hotel and waited until she left." Kent laughed again. "Killing Dwayne Dailey was the easiest thing I've ever done."

"Maybe," Anthony said tersely, "but not the smartest. Chuck"—Anthony turned to his friend—"did you get all that?"

Sergeant Chuck Robinson of the Detroit Police Department approached the pair with his handcuffs ready. "Yep, every word." Chuck closed in and swiftly handcuffed the now sobbing man.

"Kent Julian, you are under arrest for the murder of Dwayne Dailey. You have the right to remain silent . . ."

Anthony's face split into the first truly joyous smile he'd had since Savannah had been arrested. He watched as Chuck led the killer to a waiting police car. Unable to wait another moment, he rushed to

the nearest pay phone and called Zane Reeves. Zane
answered on the second ring.

"Reeves! We've got him!" Anthony was practically
screaming into the phone.

"Wait a minute, Martin. Calm down! You've got
what?"

"The killer! We caught him!"

"How do you know?"

"He confessed, Reeves! We've got a taped confession. We have him! He's a former employee of Savannah's, a man named Kent Julian."

"What?" Zane jumped out of his chair. He could
start to feel some of Anthony's excitement reach
through the phone to infect him. "Are you sure
about this?"

"Of course I'm sure," Anthony yelled. "He confessed, I'm telling you. I have it on tape!"

"I don't know how much good a taped confession
is going to be," Zane said.

"But one of my buddies from the Detroit police
force was with me. He heard the whole thing. Kent
Julian followed Savannah to New Orleans and then
killed Dailey after she left. I'm telling you, I have the
whole thing on tape!"

Zane processed that information for a moment.
"That is amazing news," he said. "I'm going to get
right on this."

"So you'll let her go now, right?" Anthony demanded. "You're going to set her free?"

"Well, there are some legalities that I'll have to
work through," Zane noted. "And we typically like
to get the actual killer before we release the person
we have in custody."

"What are you saying? A bird in the hand is worth

two in the bush?" Anthony was outraged. "Do you mean Savannah is going to have to wait in jail until you can get up here to extradite Julian to New Orleans?"

"Wait a minute, let me think." Zane was quiet for a moment. "There may be another way to do this. Sit tight, Martin. I'm going to make a few calls and rattle a few cages to see what I can do. I'll get right back with you. This was really excellent work."

"Zane, you don't know how happy I am," Anthony said.

"Yes, I do," Zane assured him. "Have you talked to Mrs. Dailey's sister yet?" Zane asked casually.

"Which sister?" Anthony was momentarily confused.

"The one that's here—Jakarta?"

"No, man, I called you first," Anthony answered.

"Would you like me to give her a call?"

Anthony smiled on his end of the phone, catching a tone in Zane's voice that he recognized. "Yeah, sure, that'd be great. I'll call her sisters here."

"Good work, Martin," Zane said again.

"Now you get to do your part, Reeves," Anthony said. "Hurry up and get Savannah home." He hung up the phone.

Thrilled by this development, Zane immediately began making phone calls and starting on the paperwork that would need to be processed before Savannah could be released. He was able to schedule a hearing for the next morning.

"Fast-tracked," he said ironically, thinking back to his earlier conversation with his boss. After the hearing was set, he flipped through the Dailey file on his desk and found the phone number for the hotel where Jakarta Raven was staying. He hesitated for a moment, and then made the call. He was connected to her room, and Jakarta answered.

"Ms. Raven, this is Zane Reeves in the prosecutor's office."

Jakarta snapped to attention. "Yes, Mr. Reeves, what's going on? Has something happened with my sister?"

"Yes, as a matter of fact it has," Zane said, "and it's wonderful news I thought you'd want to hear right away."

"So tell me," she urged.

"Your detective friend in Detroit was able to find and capture the real killer."

"What?" Jakarta shrieked. "Are you saying Savannah can go now?"

"Well, it's not quite that simple," Zane said. "We have to have a hearing—"

"Another hearing?" Jakarta interrupted. "How long will that take?"

"I've gotten it scheduled for tomorrow morning," Zane assured her. "The hearing is tomorrow morning, and if what Martin tells me is correct, your sister can be out and on her way home by lunch tomorrow."

"Oh, my gosh, that is incredible news!" Jakarta felt tears begin to well up in her eyes. "Thank you so much."

"I didn't do much of anything," Zane said. "You need to be sure to thank that detective of yours."

"Does Savannah know yet?"

"Her lawyer has been notified, and he may have been in to see her already. I'm not sure."

"Well, I'm going over there right now," Jakarta declared.

"Um . . . aren't visiting hours over?" he asked.

"Damn, you're right." Jakarta sounded frustrated. "Oh, I want to see her!"

"Well, let me see if there isn't something I can do," Zane said. "Stay by the phone, I'll call you right back."

Zane quickly made another call to a friend at the jailhouse. "I need to see one of the inmates tonight."

"This is highly unusual, Mr. Reeves," the guard said.

"I know, but this is an unusual circumstance. I need to see Savannah Dailey. I'll only need about a half hour."

"Well, I suppose it would be okay," the guard said hesitantly.

"Excellent. I'm on my way, and I'll be bringing someone with me." Zane hung up before the guard could protest.

When he called Jakarta back, she answered on the first ring. "I got us in to see her, but we only have a half hour and we have to go right now," he said.

"Great, I'll meet you at the jail," Jakarta said.

"No," he said, "your hotel is on my way. I'll come by and pick you up."

Jakarta agreed. "I'll be in the lobby waiting."

When Zane arrived, Jakarta was ready to go. She hopped into his car and they sped off toward the jail.

"I really appreciate this," she said. "I can't believe this whole thing is almost over."

Zane nodded. "I knew the system would work."

Jakarta made a harrumphing sound in her throat.

"Don't get me started talking about the system. You won't like what I have to say."

Zane chuckled. "No, I guess I wouldn't at that."

They arrived at the jail and Zane used his special parking permit to get them right at the door. He led the way inside and after a quick ID check at the entrance, Zane and Jakarta were led to the counsel room.

"I've never been here before," Jakarta said.

"You wouldn't have been," Zane answered. "This is where the inmates meet with their attorneys."

At that moment, Savannah was led in, a dumb-struck look on her face. When she saw her sister, Savannah ran to her.

"Oh, my God, did you hear? It's over! I'm going to go home!" Savannah was laughing and crying at the same time.

"I know, Zane told me." Jakarta wrapped her sister in a bear hug, the first physical contact they'd had in weeks. "It's finally over. Anthony found the killer."

"Who was it?" Savannah asked. "My lawyer wasn't sure." Both women looked in Zane's direction.

"I don't know all the details—Martin will have to give you those—but I understand the killer is a former employee of yours, a Kent Julian," Zane replied.

"Kent?" Savannah looked shocked. "But why . . ."

"It doesn't matter," Jakarta insisted. "All that matters is that he confessed, and you're going to get to go home soon. Zane said it could be as early as tomorrow!"

"Tomorrow . . ." Savannah seemed overwhelmed by the enormity of it all. "I can be with my children tomorrow."

Soon, the visit was over and Zane and Jakarta had to leave.

"I'll see you at the hearing tomorrow, sis," Jakarta said. "And hopefully, we'll catch a flight home tomorrow afternoon."

Anthony had caught the first available flight out of Detroit to New Orleans, wanting to be on hand to escort Savannah home. Once Zane had the official evidence of Kent Julian's confession, he was able to process all the necessary paperwork to drop the charges and release Savannah from custody. The hearing went smoothly. No complications or technicalities stood in the way of Savannah's release.

When Savannah left the New Orleans jail, there was a small welcoming party on hand to greet her. Jakarta could barely contain her joy. As soon as Savannah emerged from the lockup, Jakarta ran to her and buried her sister in a bear hug. Savannah was dumbfounded by the speed of it all.

"How did this all happen?" she asked Jakarta.

"I don't exactly know. Anthony will tell us all about it on the flight home. It's over, do you understand that? It's over!" Jakarta was crying tears of joy. The sisters hugged intensely.

When Savannah released her sister, the only face she saw was Anthony's. She approached him slowly, as if afraid that moving too fast would cause him to evaporate like a heat mirage.

"You saved my life," she said. "I don't know how you did it, but you saved my life." She reached out to him and wrapped her arms around his neck, pulling him closer. He placed his hands on the sides of her face, touching the smooth softness with wonder, making up for all the time they'd lost.

"I'm never going to let you go again," he said.

Savannah's spirit felt lighter than the air around them. She couldn't believe the ordeal was over, she couldn't believe she was back in his strong arms, and she couldn't believe that soon she would be back in her house with her family.

"It's all happening too fast," she said. "How did this happen?"

"Later, baby," he promised, "I'll tell you the whole story later." Anthony dipped his head and tasted her lips. They kissed as though they were all alone. They kissed as though they could erase the recent trauma with the sheer force of their passion.

Standing a few respectful feet back, Jakarta and Zane watched the touching reunion.

"Thank you," Jakarta said to him.

"You don't have to thank me. Anthony did the hard part."

"No, I know you gave him information and guidance." Jakarta looked him in the eye. "And I just want you to know how much I appreciate it."

"All I ever wanted was justice," Zane insisted.

By then, Savannah and Anthony had joined them.

"Thank you, Mr. Reeves." Savannah shook his hand.

Zane shrugged. "As I was just telling your sister, Anthony did the hard part."

"Oh, I'll be thanking him later." Savannah smiled.

Twenty-four

Jakarta had called Detroit and let the family know what was going on, so when their plane arrived from New Orleans, the scene at the airport was pure pandemonium.

When Savannah emerged from the plane, she was overwhelmed by the veritable forest of balloons and flowers.

"Mommy! Welcome home!" Stephanie's voice was the first one she heard.

Savannah rushed to her children and pulled them into her arms. She cried freely, openly, so very happy to be back in the arms of her family.

"Tell me how you guys are doing," she said to her children.

"A hundred thousand times better now, Mom," D.J. answered, "now that you're home."

Sydney and Paris stood back as long as they could bear, and then rushed to join in on the hugs. The airport terminal became Raven Family Central as they all embraced and hugged and cried together.

Paris insisted on a big family dinner to celebrate Savannah's homecoming.

"After all this prison food, I can't think of anything I'd rather do," Savannah giggled.

"Anthony, you will join us, right?" Paris asked him.

"Yes, of course I will," Anthony said, flattered to have been invited.

Dinner was a loud and joyous affair with everyone so excited to have the family reunited. Anthony told the whole story about Dwayne's murder, leaving out the information he'd found out about Dwayne's affairs. He'd decided he would give Savannah that information privately at some other time and let her decide how much, if any, she wanted to share with her sisters and children.

Sydney was especially happy to have Savannah home because it meant she could return the reins of Dailey Plumbing.

"I did the best I could," Sydney told her sister. "And the business is okay, but I never quite developed the right touch with the plumbers."

Savannah smiled at her sister and kissed her cheek. "I'm just glad that you were willing to try," she said. "But you're right—you're not a plumbers' kind of girl."

Sydney shrugged. "I am what I am." She laughed.

The dinner lasted well into the night, with no one willing to break up the party. As everyone was eating dessert, Savannah tapped on her wineglass with a fork, silencing everyone.

"There are a couple of things I want to say. First of all, I think you all have to know how much your love and support has meant to me over these months." Savannah's voice was thick with emotion. "And I know without a shadow of a doubt that I would not have been able to make it through this without my family by my side, and for that I love you all. I have grown a lot during this time and it's amazing what quiet time in jail will do for your thought processes."

A slight titter of laughter rippled through the room.

"So, I've made a decision, and I think it's the right thing to do," Savannah continued, "and I hope you all agree."

"What's on your mind, Savannah?" Paris asked.

"I would like for us to have a memorial service for Dwayne." Savannah studied their reactions closely.

"What?" Sydney said, voicing the outrage that showed on the faces of almost everyone around the table. "A memorial service? You mean as in 'good riddance, you dog'?"

"No." Savannah shook her head. "And whatever else Dwayne did, he was first and foremost Stephanie and D.J.'s father." She turned to her children. "This all has to have been almost as hard for you as it's been for me. It cannot have been easy for you listening to everyone talk about your father as if he were some kind of monster."

Although they fidgeted uncomfortably in their chairs, the children didn't answer.

"But the truth of the matter is we've all suffered a terrible loss," Savannah continued. "Dwayne was a part of our family for seventeen years. Whatever he did and whatever he became, he was a part of us. We owe it to the memory of what he was and to what we all were together to end it with some dignity and grace."

Jakarta shook her head. "I don't understand why

you want to do this, Savannah. After all you've been through because of that man, why would you want to memorialize him?"

"Most of the things you're referring to have only happened in the last year," Savannah pointed out. "We can't just ignore everything that came before that. And I wouldn't presume to speak for any of you, but I need the opportunity to say good-bye."

The room fell quiet as each person weighed the power and truth of Savannah's words.

"Well, how is that even possible?" Sydney demanded finally. "I thought Dwayne had been cremated in New Orleans."

"Obviously we're not going to have a burial, because you're right about the cremation," Savannah conceded. "But we can still say good-bye with a little dignity. We'll have a simple service at a chapel, maybe just the family and a few close friends."

Savannah turned to Anthony, a pleading look on her face. "You're outside of the family; do you think this is a crazy idea?" she asked.

He shook his head. "No, I don't. I think it's a beautiful loving gesture. It shows who you are and what you're about. And if there's something you need me to do to help, I will."

"Thank you for that." Savannah smiled at him. "Now let's plan to do this soon. I'm going to call a chapel tomorrow and make arrangements for as soon as possible."

"Whatever you think is best, Savannah," Sydney said. "I still don't think Dwayne deserves this kind of honor and respect from us, but I will certainly support your decision."

"Thank you, Syd." Savannah nodded.

When finally the meal was over and the dishes cleared, Sydney and Paris prepared to go.

"I guess I don't have to stay here tonight." Paris yawned.

"Thank you, Aunt Paris." D.J. hugged her. "Thank you for agreeing to stay here with us and help us through."

Paris wiped a tear from her eye. "Of course I agreed to stay. You two were wonderful. You made it the easiest thing I've ever had to do."

Savannah joined in with her children. "Thank you, Paris," she said. "One of the main things that helped me remain sane through this whole ordeal was the knowledge that my children were absolutely safe and that you were taking care of them."

Paris assured her. "It's what sisters do for each other."

"I'm coming to find out that list of 'what sisters do for each other' is apparently endless." Savannah smiled through unshed tears.

Twenty-five

The memorial service was scheduled for two days later. Savannah envisioned the service as being brief and private, and she hoped the ceremony and ritual of the event would bring her family some peace. She notified all of the employees, friends, and business contacts who she thought might be interested. She could tell from the response she got when she made the calls that many people thought she was out of her mind. But she had no doubts that it was the right thing to do.

"I owe this to my children," she said to herself repeatedly. "They have to be able to say good-bye."

As she prepared for the service, she methodically went through her house, gathering up all the artifacts of Dwayne and their life together. Some of the family pictures and mementos she would have on display at the memorial service. But most of them would be packed away. Savannah had decided that for her to be able to move on with her life, she could not on a regular basis face the pictures and souvenirs of her former life.

On the day of the memorial, she was in the study cleaning out drawers in a way that she never had in the months after Dwayne left, when Stephanie approached her.

"Mom, can I talk to you for a minute?"

"Sure, baby. Come on in. What's on your mind?"

"Mom, I'm so sorry for everything Daddy put you through."

Savannah looked at her daughter curiously. "Daddy put all of us through a lot, baby. But we're getting through it."

"Here are some pictures of Daddy that I had up in my room." Stephanie held the pictures out to her mother. "You can get rid of them if you want."

Savannah's gaze traveled from the pictures to her daughter. "Oh, baby," she said and rose to wrap her daughter in a hug. "You don't have to get rid of your pictures of your daddy. I know you loved him. If you want to remember him like this"—Savannah looked down at the smiling, charming face of the Dwayne Dailey she used to know—"you do that."

"But you've cleared all the others out," Stephanie said, looking at the box on the floor.

"I had to do that for me," Savannah answered. "In the parts of the house where I'm going to be living and working, removing these pictures was something I had to do for my piece of mind. But I know that your memories are your memories. I wouldn't ask you to get rid of them and I wouldn't try to take them away from you. I love you and I wish I could do or say something that would make all this unpleasantness go away, but I can't. So if having pictures of your daddy around you will help, then you keep all the pictures you want."

Stephanie fiercely hugged her mother. "I feel like I'm being unfair to you by holding on to memories of Daddy."

"My relationship with your father does not have to

have anything to do with your relationship with your father. I believe he loved you, and my wish for you is that you remember him that way."

"How can you be so calm about this?" Stephanie demanded suddenly. "He ran out on us, you wound up in jail accused of killing him. How can you still be so calm?"

Savannah took a moment to try and answer that question in a way that would make sense to her now fourteen-year-old daughter. "Baby, I believe that everything in life happens for a reason. I believe whatever happens was supposed to happen as a part of the divine order of things. I believe that if I don't question my blessings, then I can't question my trials. And while I'm not exactly sure why we had this trial, I know it's part of something greater. And knowing that is what gets me through and what stops me from being filled with hatred for your father."

Stephanie shook her head. "That's pretty deep, Mom."

"Hey, prison'll do that to you," Savannah joked. "Now shouldn't you be getting ready? We're going to have to leave for the chapel soon."

"Yes, ma'am."

"Where's your brother, Steph? I haven't seen much of him today? How's he doing with all this?"

"I don't know, Mom. D.J. has never quite understood why this all happened."

Savannah nodded. "I don't think I'm going to be able to help him with that," she said. "But I'll try." Savannah kissed her daughter on her cheek and then sent her on her way.

She left her task of clearing away the memory of

Dwayne to go in search of her son. She found him in his bedroom sitting on the edge of the bed with a Little League baseball trophy in his hands.

Savannah knocked softly on the door. "What's up, D.J.? Shouldn't you be getting dressed?"

"Daddy was my coach the year we won this." D.J. held the trophy out toward her. "We had so much fun that year. Me and Daddy used to go out for pizza after the games—you remember that, Mom?"

"Yes, D.J., I remember." Savannah entered the room and sat on the bed next to him.

"On the games that we won, Daddy always bought the whole team ice cream." D.J. smiled at the memory. "We were the Dailey Plumbing Tigers," D.J. said proudly.

"I remember," Savannah said. "I remember every game. You guys were really good."

"Mommy, how did all this happen? How did the same person who coached my Little League team and took us all out for ice cream after the game do something like that? What happened?"

"I don't know, baby. I don't think we're ever really going to have an answer to that now that your daddy's gone."

"It's just so unfair," D.J. said quietly. "What did I do?"

"What makes you think did anything?" Savannah asked, confused. "Why do you think this has anything to do with you?"

"Something made him leave, Mom," D.J. said.

"I think that something had everything to do with him, not us." Savannah replied. "I think that something was a part of his soul and didn't have anything to do with us and there was nothing we could have done to stop it."

"Do you really believe that?" D.J. demanded.

"I have to or else I'll go insane because there is no way to know otherwise."

"I really miss him, Mom."

"I know you do, baby, and that's okay. He'll always be a part of you. But today we have to go and say good-bye."

D.J. nodded and got up from the bed to get his clothes out of the closet. Savannah rose and started to leave the room so he could get dressed.

"So why did Mr. Julian kill Daddy?" D.J. blurted out. "What did he have against Daddy?"

Savannah paused with one hand clasping the doorknob, lowered her head, and rubbed the bridge of her nose. After a moment she turned back to face her son.

"I guess it's all going to come out in the trial anyway." Savannah sighed. "Your father was having an affair with Mr. Julian's wife and Mr. Julian was very angry about both the affair and having lost his job at Dailey Plumbing."

"Daddy was having an affair?" D.J. was stunned.

"Yes, sweetheart. Mrs. Julian was only one of several women your father had affairs with."

"I didn't know," D.J. said quietly.

Savannah shook her head. "Neither did I, baby, and I'm the one who should have. But we can't beat ourselves up about this. All we can do is move on."

D.J. nodded in agreement. "So"—D.J. looked at his mother—"are you going to be going out with Mr. Martin now?"

Savannah looked her son in the eye. "Yes, baby, I

am. I like Anthony a lot. He's a really nice guy who's been really good to me. He saved my life by getting me out of that prison. So yes, D.J., I am going to go out with him." Savannah braced herself for his reaction.

"Okay, it's cool," D.J. responded. He turned his attention to getting ready for the memorial service.

Savannah breathed a sigh of relief and left D.J. to his preparations.

The chapel Savannah found for the service was small but elegant. At the front of the room by the altar was an eight-by-ten framed photograph of Dwayne with D.J. and Stephanie on either side, the resemblance on their smiling faces clearly evident, the picture obviously taken at a much happier time. There was a small wreath at the base of the easel and across the wreath a gold ribbon with the words *Goodbye, Daddy* written in glitter. Savannah was surprised when she entered the chapel to find other floral arrangements there as well. She walked to the front to inspect the gift cards on the flowers. She was surprised to see floral tributes from a couple of their suppliers and clients. But the floral arrangement that surprised her the most was a tall spray of roses and greenery that stood next to the photograph. The card read. *For everything you were, Sydney, Paris, and Jakarta.* Savannah's eyes welled up with tears, touched by the thoughtfulness of her sisters. Anthony joined her at the front, near the floral arrangements.

"I guess this was a really good idea," Anthony said quietly.

She reached for his hand. "I sure hope so. I sure hope I'm doing the right thing," Savannah replied.

"I'm certain that you're doing the right thing for your children," he said. "Nobody else really matters."

Savannah smiled gratefully at him. "Thank you for saying that. You're a good man to have around, Charlie Brown," she teased.

Other mourners started to arrive as Savannah took a seat in the pew between her children. Anthony sat in the pew directly behind them. The small chapel quickly began to fill with faces that surprised Savannah. There were some employees of Dailey Plumbing, there were customers of Dailey Plumbing, there were a couple of women that Savannah didn't know. However, based on what had been revealed to her about Dwayne's life, she could speculate on who those women might be. She supposed that she should have been angry, outraged even, by the nerve of these women to show up at her husband's memorial service, but she wasn't. *They have as much right to say good-bye to Dwayne as anybody,* she decided. Her sisters came in hesitantly, apparently not completely resigned to attending the memorial service. They sat in the pew next to Anthony.

"How long do you suppose this dog and pony show is going to last?" Sydney asked impatiently.

"It'll last as long as it takes," Savannah hissed. "Now, behave. We've come this far, just tough it out."

Sydney rolled her eyes and settled back against the pew. It was a much longer event than Savannah had anticipated. Because of the way Dwayne's life ended, Savannah expected some degree of curiosity and rubbernecking, but to her pleasant surprise, most of the mourners seemed to genuinely want to pay their respects, if not to Dwayne, then certainly to his family. So, as she and the children sat in the front pew, many people filed past sharing thoughts, a word of condolence, or a memory of Dwayne from days gone by. Eventually the chaplain of the small chapel approached Savannah's pew.

"We can begin whenever you are ready," he said to her.

Savannah nodded and said a few words of thanks to the person in front of her. She squeezed each of her children's hands firmly and then rose to approach the front of the chapel. As people noticed her standing there, the room began to quiet down and the mourners settled into their seats.

"Ladies and gentlemen, my name is Savannah Raven Dailey. I would to thank you all for taking time out of your busy schedules to come here today to join us as we say good-bye to Dwayne Dailey."

Savannah could not, in her soul, despite how forgiving she wanted to be, manage to say the words "my husband" before Dwayne's name.

"This has been a very difficult time for my entire family," she said. "And it has been made even more difficult by the circumstances surrounding Dwayne's death. As I'm sure you all know by now, those circumstances were tragic and devastating, but it in no way diminishes our need to bid Dwayne good-bye. So it's in that spirit and in the memory of the person that he was and the man that we'll all remember that we have gathered here to say good-bye. Dwayne was a unique man with many strengths and many weaknesses but what will always remain in my mind when I think of Dwayne was his unparalleled love for his children." She then smiled at Stephanie and D.J. "They will always be Dwayne's legacy. So for the blessing that is my children and for the gift that is their lives I will always thank you, Dwayne, and always be grateful that you came into my life."

Savannah lowered her head, struggling to fight back the tears that threatened to burst out at any second. After a moment she composed herself. "If anyone else has anything else they would like to say, please feel free to come forward now." She then took her seat next to her children.

Stephanie reached over and hugged her mother; and D.J., wanting desperately to be cool as all six-teen-year-old boys do, could only manage to squeeze her hand. The chapel was still and silent for a moment as no one else approached the front. After a few strained moments, D.J. stood and approached the front. The room was totally silent as the young man made his way to the front and took his place next to the picture of his father.

"This has been the worst thing that has ever happened to me," D.J. said. "Because I loved my father. My father was my hero. I thought he could do anything, fix anything, be anything. I thought he was Superman. The past year has taught me a lot about heroes, and it has shown me what a hero is really made of. So even though I loved my dad and I will always hold onto the memories of the man that I knew as a kid, I know now what a true hero is."

D.J. walked to his mother and held her hand. "Mom is my hero," he said. "Mom held us all together and fought through things that nobody should have to deal with. And throughout the whole thing, she was always loving, kind, and strong for my sister and me. Even when I was mean to her, Mom never let me down. So I come to say good-bye to my dad, and to let my mom know how much I love her, how much I believe in her, and how very grateful I am that she is my mom."

Savannah cried openly then, no longer attempting to hold back the tears. She rose from her pew and embraced her son as she wept. The whole family crowded around, hugging and crying intensely, the first true moment of mourning any of them had had since Dwayne's death. After D.J. sat down, several other mourners moved to the front of the chapel, each wanting to tell of a happy memory or a significant moment they'd shared with Dwayne. When the memorial service finally ended, Savannah was drained but happy.

"It went well, sis," Sydney said to her after everyone had left. "I thought it was a crazy thing to do, but apparently a lot of people, not just us, needed to say good-bye to Dwayne."

"It reaffirms the life that we lived," Savannah said. "It ended badly; there's never going to be any doubt about that. But this memorial service reaffirms that it was a good life for a really long time."

Sydney nodded and hugged her sister. "Now you get to move on to maybe a better life," she said, raising her eyebrow at a sight across the room.

Savannah turned to see what had attracted her sister's attention and saw Anthony and D.J. deep in conversation. "Wonder what that's about," she said.

"That was a beautiful thing you did for your mother," Anthony said to D.J. "She really needed that."

"I meant every word," D.J. assured him. "Mom's been a rock and I've treated her badly. I wanted to apologize for that."

"I think she understands."

"I've been mean to you too, Mr. Martin," D.J. said. "Maybe not mean to you directly, but I really resisted having you in our lives. I didn't think it was right."

"I know and I understood how you felt." Anthony nodded.

"But I want to apologize to you too. My mother is happy with you," D.J. said. "Happier than I remember seeing her in a really long time. And if she's happy, then that's all that really matters to me." D.J. held his hand out to shake. Anthony took the boy's hand firmly. "I don't know what your relationship is with my mother, but I want you to know that it's okay with me, whatever it is."

Anthony shook his hand. "Thank you. And I want you to know that I am not trying to replace your dad in your life, but if you ever need to talk about anything, I'm here." D.J. nodded gratefully.

Savannah, who had been watching their exchange from across the room, approached them slowly. "We need to head out of here, guys," she said. "Are you ready to go?"

D.J. nodded. "Yes, ma'am; it's time."

Stephanie, having retrieved the photograph from the easel in front of the chapel, joined them and the four of them left the chapel together.

Twenty-six

By the time they reached Savannah's house, it had grown late in the evening. Drained from the emotional events of the day, the children said their good nights and immediately retreated to their rooms.

Once they were alone, Savannah took Anthony by the hand. She led him through her house, up the stairs, and to her bedroom. Anthony followed silently, allowing Savannah to take charge. In her bedroom, she closed and locked the door, and turned to face him.

"I want you to stay tonight." She held his hand. "I need to be with you. I've wanted to be with you ever since I got home from New Orleans, but I knew I had to close the chapter on Dwayne before I could move forward."

"And have you? Is the chapter closed?" Anthony unconsciously held his breath waiting for her answer.

"Yes," she said firmly. "The memorial service today brought me much more peace than I ever expected. And I knew that I would never be able to come to you with an open mind and heart until that was finished. So yes, the Dwayne chapter is finished." She met his eyes. "Will you stay the night with me?"

"Are you sure? What about the kids? Wouldn't you rather go to my place?"

Savannah shook her head. "No, I need to be home. I need to sleep in my own bed." She leaned over and kissed him lightly. "And I need you."

He cupped her face with his hand and lightly stroked her cheek with his thumb. She nuzzled into his hand, savoring the feel of his strength against her softness.

"I had a lot of time to think in jail, and I realized that one of the first things I'd have to do to reclaim my life would be to chase the memory of Dwayne out of my house. I even thought about selling the house and moving, but I'm not going to do that . . . this is my house. I do, however, need to replace the unpleasant memories with new ones." She pressed her body against his. "I'd like to start in my bedroom," she said in a husky whisper.

Anthony's body responded to her invitation long before he could engage his brain. Instinctively, he gathered her in his arms and kissed her fiercely. These were no tender reunion kisses. These were kisses that told of raw need, naked desire. Their lips and tongues demanded and gave, conquered and submitted with an ever-rising passion.

Clothes were discarded in a frenzy of movement with no regard for niceties like buttons. In very short order, they stood eye-to-eye, heart-to-heart, and toe-to-toe, each reveling in the sensual awareness of the other.

Savannah inhaled deeply of the clean, fresh smell of Anthony's skin. She ran her hands slowly across his back, down his arms, and over his rear, marveling at the tightly coiled strength of his muscles. She savored the taste of him, planting soft kisses and leaving a trail of fire everywhere on his body her lips touched. She traced the edges of his nipple with the tip of her tongue and smiled when she heard his sharp intake of breath. She moved her kisses even lower on his body until she reached the juncture of his powerful legs where his manhood stood proudly erect.

She slid her tongue along the length of him. Anthony gasped for air and grabbed her shoulders for support. Savannah was deliberately slow in her ministrations, licking his shaft first along one side and then down the other with exquisite patience. And then she guided his penis into her mouth, fully encasing him with moist warmth. Anthony groaned and struggled to keep his knees from buckling under him.

After a few minutes of her divine suckling, he could take no more. "I need to be inside you, now," he moaned. Savannah moved just far enough away from him to gently push him back onto her bed. She padded silently across the room and entered her bathroom. After a moment, she emerged with a foil package in her hand.

"I stopped by the store earlier today," she said. "I knew I was going to need this tonight." She climbed onto the bed next to where he lay on his back and slowly tore open the package. She eased the condom into place, watching his eyes as passion, fire, and need shimmered in the green depths.

"I felt so out of control of my life during this whole experience, going all the way back to when Dwayne disappeared," Savannah whispered. "But it's over now, and now I need to regain control."

"So this is all about control?" he asked.

"Not all," she conceded. "It's also all about you and me."

She straddled him and eased herself down onto his throbbing shaft. Powerful beams of erotic pleasure shot through her body all emanating from their point of joining. Savannah shuddered from the force of the sensations wracking her body. She moved in a frenzy, as if chasing after an elusive goal that was so tantalizingly out of reach. The deliberate slowness with which she had begun this encounter was gone, burned off in the white-hot heat of her need. Anthony matched her pace and tempo with a need of his own. Together they rocketed toward fulfillment. When the moment came, it was as if a star had exploded within them, sending billions of sparkling particles throughout their bodies until even the tips of their fingers and toes tingled with pleasure.

Spent, Savannah collapsed against his chest. He wrapped his arms around her and held her there, whispering words of love into her ear.

Eventually, she eased off his body and moved to lie next to him.

"I don't even know where to start thanking you," she said. "You absolutely saved my life."

"I think you saved my life," he responded.

"What are you talking about?"

"I was lost and alone until you came into my life," he said softly, "and you saved me from that."

Savannah smiled. "This is more of a blessing than I ever imagined or dared pray for. The whole time I was in jail, with all that time on my hands to think, my thoughts kept coming back to you. And I wondered what would become of us if I got out of jail."

"If you got out of jail? You questioned whether or

not you would get out of jail?" Anthony was surprised.

"Every day," she said. "But when I allowed myself
to think about life outside of jail, I thought about a
life with you. And . . ."

"And?" he prompted.

"And I honestly don't know what the future is
going to bring. I'm just getting my life back and
there are so many things I have to reconnect with.
But I do hope and pray that whatever my life becomes now, you'll be a part of it."

Anthony leaned toward her and kissed her. It was
a tender kiss, filled with the promise of the future.
As Savannah responded to his kiss, tears rolled down
her face.

"Why are you crying?" he asked.

"I don't ever remember being this happy, feeling
this content, being this secure, or feeling this loved
before," she sniffled. "Thank you for everything
you've brought to my life."

"Stick around." Anthony smiled. "The best is yet
to come."

Dear Readers:

When Savannah came to me, I wondered how a woman could overcome what has to be one of the worst kinds of betrayal a husband can do to a wife. The story began for me with the question "What if?" What do you do if you wake up one morning and your whole world has been turned upside down? What do you do if just when you think you've gotten your life back on track, it flips again? And what do you do if in the midst of the turmoil, fate intervenes and brings in the man who could possibly be the great love of your life? LOVE'S DESTINY is my look at how one woman—one family—deals with a life-altering event. I hope you enjoyed Savannah and Anthony's story as much as I enjoyed writing it.

One of Savannah's biggest assets, of course, is her family. Her sisters, each with her own strength, provide the support Savannah needs to go on. I'm going to be spending some time with Jakarta, the wild Raven sister, next. I can hardly wait to see how her story turns out! I hope you'll join me.

Best wishes,
Crystal Wilson-Harris

ABOUT THE AUTHOR

Romance novelist Crystal Wilson-Harris is an Associate Professor of Developmental English at Sinclair Community College in her hometown of Dayton, Ohio. She holds a bachelor's degree from Howard University in Washington, D.C., and a master's degree from the University of Dayton.

Her first novel, DARK EMBRACE, was released in 1991 by Odyssey Books and rereleased in 1997 by Genesis Press. Arabesque Books has released her subsequent novels: THE ART OF LOVE (1997), CHERISH (1998), MASQUERADE (2000), and GOOD INTENTIONS (2001). Her books have been well received, with GOOD INTENTIONS being given the Award of Merit from the Romance in Color Web site.

Crystal enjoys spending time with her family and volunteering in various community service organizations. Her other interests include jazz, cyberspace, auto racing (watching, not driving—yet), a not-so-secret affinity for all things *Star Trek* (*Next Generation* only, please), and an almost obsessive love for home improvement/decorating programs.

Despite a schedule that has her juggling a full-time job, two kids, a dog, and a cat, Crystal is currently hard at work on her next book, the second in the series *The Raven Sisters—Women of Destiny.*

Crystal loves to hear from other lovers of great romance. She invites you to contact her via E-mail at crystalwh@netzero.net or snail mail at P.O. Box 60702, Dayton, Ohio 45406 (please include a self-addressed, stamped envelope).

COMING IN MAY 2002 FROM
ARABESQUE ROMANCES

More Sizzling Romance From
Leslie Esdaile

More Sizzling Romance From
Marcia King-Gamble

__**Reason to Love**   1-58314-133-2   **$5.99**US/**$7.99**CAN

__**Illusions of Love**   1-58314-104-9   **$5.99**US/**$7.99**CAN

__**Under Your Spell**   1-58314-027-1   **$4.99**US/**$6.50**CAN

__**Eden's Dream**   0-7860-0572-6   **$4.99**US/**$6.50**CAN

__**Remembrance**   0-7860-0504-1   **$4.99**US/**$6.50**CAN

Call toll free **1-888-345-BOOK** to order by phone or use this coupon to order by mail.
Name_____
Address_____
City_____ State_____ Zip_____
Please send me the books I have checked above.
I am enclosing $_____
Plus postage and handling* $_____
Sales tax (in NY, TN, and DC) $_____
Total amount enclosed $_____
*Add $2.50 for the first book and $.50 for each additional book.
Send check or money order (no cash or CODs) to: **Arabesque Books, Dept. C.O. 850 Third Avenue, 16th Floor, New York, NY 10022**
Prices and numbers subject to change without notice.
All orders subject to availability.
Visit our website at **www.arabesquebooks.com**.

More Sizzling Romance by
Gwynne Forster

__**Beyond Desire**   1-58314-201-0   **$5.99**US/**$7.99**CAN

Amanda Ross is thrilled when she is appointed the principal of a school but scared that her out-of-wedlock pregnancy will cost her the promotion. She needs a husband, fast, and that's where Marcus Hickson comes in. But this marriage of convenience may soon become an affair of the heart . . .

__**Fools Rush In**   1-58314-037-9   **$4.99**US/**$6.99**CAN

When Justine Montgomery gave up her baby, she never knew how badly she would regret her decision. After going incognito, she's found the child—and the man who adopted her. Now, amidst divided loyalties and an unexpected passion, Justine must risk it all to claim a love she never thought possible . . .

__**Obsession**   1-58314-092-1   **$5.99**US/**$7.99**CAN

Selena Sutton left her promising career to return home to Texas and found love with Magnus Cooper. But Magnus's spoiled playboy of a brother, Cooper, is obsessed with her, and now the couple must trust in each other—and their love—in order to triumph.

__**Sealed With A Kiss**   0-7860-0189-5   **$4.99**US/**$5.99**CAN

Nothing drives Naomi Logan crazier than sexist radio host Rufus Meade. But after telling him what she thinks about his views—on air—the last thing she expects is to see him standing on her doorstep . . . handsome, outspoken, and extremely sexy.

Call toll free **1-888-345-BOOK** to order by phone or use this coupon to order by mail.

Name_____

Address_____

City_____ State_____ Zip_____

Please send me the books that I checked above.

I am enclosing $_____

Plus postage and handling* $_____

Sales tax (in NY, TN, and DC) $_____

Total amount enclosed $_____

*Add $2.50 for the first book and $.50 for each additional book.

Send check or money order (no cash or CODs) to: **Arabesque Books, Dept. C.O., 850 Third Avenue, 16th Floor, New York, NY 10022**

Prices and numbers subject to change without notice.

All orders subject to availability.

Visit our website at **www.arabesquebooks.com.**